THE EPIC OF EIRIK BLOODAXE

HILMARJ TORGRIM

MANDOLIN PUBLISHING
Published by the Mandolin Publishing Group

Some names and characteristics of people mentioned have been changed, most events have been compressed. Randomly italicized words are for author emphasis <u>only</u>. While this story is based on the real life of the main character, it is a fictional story told through the perspective of the main character. Places, depictions, descriptions and names may have been changed for the sake of the story.

CHAPTER 1
Blood Moon Born

The howl of the north wind tore through the fjords like a beast starved for prey. Ice clung to the jagged cliffs, and the sea was a black, roiling mass, foaming like the maw of Fenrir. The night sky hung low, thick with clouds, blotting out the moon and stars. But in the great hall of Harald Fairhair, warmth and fire danced, casting long shadows over the faces of men who lived and died by the sword. Inside, the air was thick with mead and sweat, the sweet tang of blood never far from the memory of their last raid.

Harald sat at the head of the feasting table, the weight of the crown heavy on his brow. The first King of Norway, the man who had united warring chieftains under his iron rule, was a giant of a man, his chest broad like the trunk of an ancient oak, his hair—once fair and golden—now streaked with the gray of many winters. Around him were his men, hard-faced warriors, eyes glinting in the firelight. Their hands, calloused and stained from battle, clutched wooden cups of mead as they roared with laughter and song.

But beneath their revelry, something else gnawed at the edges of the hall—a sense of anticipation, a tension woven into the very timbers of the great hall. Harald's latest wife, Ragnhild Eriksdatter, lay in a back room, her cries muffled by the thick wooden walls. She was in labor.

Ragnhild was not the first of Harald's many wives, nor would she be the last. Harald had fathered more sons than could be counted on two hands, each one a pawn in the relentless game of power and blood. But tonight was different. This child, Harald felt, would be the one to carry forward his legacy—not just as a king, but as a man forged in the fire of war.

As another shriek from the birthing room echoed through the hall, Harald's hand tightened around his cup. A son. It must be a son. He needed more blood, more iron, to secure what he had built. A kingdom forged by steel and flame could not be trusted to weak men or the sons of lesser women.

An old crone, half-bent with age but still sharp-eyed, shuffled out from the shadows. "The moon hides tonight, my king," she rasped, her voice like dried leaves rustling. "A blood moon, they say. A bad omen, some think."

Harald did not flinch. "Omen or no, the gods favor the strong. Only cowards fear what they cannot see."

Before the old woman could answer, the doors to the birthing room burst open, and out staggered the midwife, her face pale and slick with sweat. In her arms was a bundle, wrapped in fur. She approached the king, her steps uneven as though the weight she carried was heavier than it should be.

"Your son," she gasped, and the hall fell silent. All eyes turned to Harald.

He rose slowly, like a mountain waking from a long slumber. His shadow loomed large as he crossed the floor and stood before the midwife. Without a word, he peeled back the fur, revealing the infant beneath.

The child's face was flushed, his small fists clenched as if already preparing for battle. His head was crowned with a thin tuft of black hair, and his eyes—when they flicked open—gleamed with a cold, unsettling sharpness.

Harald nodded, satisfied. "He will be called Eirik," he declared. "Eirik Haraldsson."

The hall erupted in cheers, the men raising their cups in salute. Harald's voice cut through their noise, hard and commanding. "Eirik Bloodaxe, I name him! For he will carve his name into the world with the edge of a blade, as I have done."

Ragnhild, exhausted but still conscious, listened from her bed. She had seen the child before they'd taken him away, and though he was yet a babe, there was something unsettling about him. His cry had been silent at first, not the wail of a newborn, but a soft, almost growling sound. And his eyes—there was something dark in them, something that reminded her too much of the beasts her father had hunted in the forests. He was not the first child she had borne, but he was the first to unsettle her like this.

The midwife tried to reassure her. "He will be strong, my lady. Born on a night like this, he is destined for greatness."

Ragnhild wasn't so sure. She turned her face to the wall, her body aching from the birth. Eirik would grow, and he would be strong, but there was a shadow that clung to him already, like the night outside.

As Eirik grew, the shadow only deepened. He was not like his brothers. Where they sought adventure, he craved violence. While his brothers hunted game for sport, Eirik hunted for blood. Before the age of ten, he had killed a man—an accident, some said, during a training bout, but those who had seen it claimed otherwise. The boy had made no effort to stop, no effort to show mercy. The blood on his axe had pleased him. The name "Bloodaxe" was not given lightly.

Harald, for all his legendary strength, began to watch his son with wary eyes. Eirik's thirst for power, for dominance, was something even his father found unsettling. Yet Harald did nothing to curb it. He had taught his sons that power was to be taken, not asked for. And Eirik, more than any of his brothers, had learned the lesson well.

By the time he was fourteen, Eirik had made his first raid, burning a rival chieftain's hall to the ground. His brothers joined him, but it was Eirik's axe that swung the hardest, cutting down men like wheat. The gods smiled on him that day, or perhaps they turned their eyes away.

Harald's hall was soon filled with rumors of what the boy would become. Some whispered that Eirik was cursed, others that he was chosen by Odin himself for Valhalla's halls. But one thing was certain—he was a force, a storm on the horizon, growing darker with each passing day.

Outside, the wind howled again, but the moon still refused to show its face. The blood moon, some called it. A sign of things to come.

Inside the great hall, young Eirik sat beside his father, watching the flames dance. His small hand, not yet large enough to grasp a full sword, clenched a carving knife. His eyes, cold and sharp, gleamed with something ancient, something that had nothing to do with kingship and everything to do with blood.

And in that moment, Harald Fairhair knew one thing: his kingdom would not fall to foreign invaders or warring tribes. It would fall from within, from the shadow sitting at his right hand.

Chapter 2
Shadows of an Axe

The wind screamed across the fjord, tearing at the trees and biting into the bones of anyone foolish enough to be out in the storm. Inside Harald's hall, the fire burned high and hot, casting a dull orange glow over the gathered company. The hall was alive with the sounds of laughter, the clinking of cups, and the hum of stories told by old warriors. But in the far corner, where the shadows clung stubbornly to the edges of the firelight, a young boy sat, sharpening a small axe with a whetstone. His eyes never left the blade, the slow, deliberate motion of his hand almost hypnotic.

Eirik Bloodaxe was thirteen winters old, but there was little left of the child in him. His limbs, once wiry and awkward, had begun to harden with muscle, his shoulders broadening, his hands rough and calloused from the grip of a weapon. His face, still smooth and boyish, was a mask of quiet intensity, broken only by the occasional flicker of emotion—a tight smile here, a narrowing of the eyes there.

"Eirik!" A voice boomed from across the hall. His older brother, Ragnvald, swaggered toward him, his chest puffed out like a cockerel about to crow. "Still polishing that axe? You've been at it for an hour. Come drink with us. You're nearly a man now. Time to learn the pleasures of mead!"

Eirik's eyes flicked up, cold and unreadable. "It's not ready."

Ragnvald laughed, the sound loud and careless. He was a year older than Eirik, taller too, with the cocky confidence of a boy who believed he had his future laid out before him. "Not ready? That little thing couldn't cut a fish, let alone a man."

Eirik's hand stilled. His fingers wrapped around the handle of the axe, his knuckles turning white. "Maybe you're right," he said quietly, his voice steady. "But I could still kill you with it."

The laughter died in Ragnvald's throat, replaced by a nervous chuckle. "Always with the threats, little brother. You've got a dark soul in you, I swear. No wonder Father named you Bloodaxe."

Eirik stood, the axe hanging loosely from his hand. He was shorter than Ragnvald, but there was something in the way he carried himself that made the other boy take a step back. "You talk too much," Eirik said, stepping closer. His eyes bore into his brother's, unblinking. "One day it'll get you killed."

The tension hung thick between them, the noise of the hall fading into the background. Ragnvald shifted his weight, his hand inching toward the hilt of his sword. But then he forced a grin, shaking his head. "You're mad," he said, backing away. "Absolutely mad."

Eirik said nothing, watching as Ragnvald returned to the other boys, his laughter forced and brittle. Only when his brother's back was turned did Eirik allow himself a faint smile. He sat back down and resumed sharpening his axe, the sound of stone on steel filling the small space around him.

Time passed in the shadow of that great hall, but Eirik's reputation did not. He became a ghost among his own family—there, but never truly part of them. His brothers trained, they drank, they laughed, and they planned their futures, each one dreaming of the day they would claim their father's throne or carve out their own kingdoms. But Eirik never spoke of his plans. He kept his thoughts locked away, his ambitions a secret even from those closest to him.

It was said that he could outfight any of his brothers, though no one had ever seen him lose his temper. His victories were cold, calculated, a blade sliding between ribs without warning. While his brothers were prone to boasts and braggadocio, Eirik remained silent. And that silence unnerved them all.

The day came when Eirik could no longer be ignored. Harald Fairhair, now aging but still strong, called for a feast in honor of his sons. The kingdom had been united, but the old king knew his reign was drawing to a close. His sons were restless, eager to carve their own names into the sagas, and the future of Norway was uncertain.

The great hall was filled to bursting that night. Warriors, chieftains, and sons of noble families gathered to drink, feast, and plot. The air buzzed with the tension of men who knew they stood on the edge of history, and in the middle of it all was Harald, his towering presence commanding respect, despite the years weighing on his shoulders.

"Tonight," Harald declared, raising his cup, "we drink to the future of Norway. My sons, the blood of kings, will carry on what I have built. And when the time comes, they will each have their part to play."

Eirik sat at the edge of the table, silent as always, watching his father and brothers. The firelight flickered across his face, casting deep shadows in the hollows of his cheeks. His eyes were distant, as if he were already looking beyond the walls of the hall, beyond the mountains and seas.

Harald's gaze swept the room, falling on each of his sons in turn. When his eyes reached Eirik, there was a flicker of something—pride, perhaps, or wariness. "Eirik Bloodaxe," the old king said, his voice thick with drink. "You, my quiet son. You do not boast like the others. What is it you seek?"

The room fell silent, all eyes turning to Eirik. His brothers, Ragnvald chief among them, leaned forward, eager to hear what the silent killer would say.

Eirik raised his head slowly, meeting his father's gaze. His voice, when it came, was low and even, cutting through the quiet like a knife. "I seek what you sought, Father. Power. But not through words. Through blood."

A murmur rippled through the hall, the chieftains exchanging uneasy glances. Harald stared at his son, the firelight reflecting in his dark eyes. "Blood is easy to spill," he said carefully. "It is harder to build something from it."

Eirik smiled, a slow, deliberate curve of the lips that sent a chill through those watching. "That depends on how much blood you are willing to spill."

Harald said nothing, but his hand tightened around his cup, his knuckles white. The old king had seen many things in his lifetime—battles, betrayals, victories—but never had he felt the cold breath of fear in his chest like he did in that moment, looking into his son's eyes.

The feast continued, but the mood had shifted. The men drank and laughed, but there was a tension that hung over the hall like a storm cloud, crackling with unseen energy. And at the center of it all was Eirik, sitting quietly, sharpening his axe, his mind already far from the noise and revelry.

The next morning, as the sun crept over the snow-covered peaks, Harald summoned his sons to him. He had seen the future in Eirik's eyes, and it troubled him. Norway could not survive another bloodbath, not after all he had done to unite it.

He stood before his sons, his gaze lingering on each one in turn. Ragnvald, strong but reckless; Olaf, cunning but untested; and then Eirik, silent, watchful, like a wolf waiting in the woods.

"You are all my blood," Harald began, his voice heavy with the weight of what was to come. "But only one of you can rule when I am gone. I will not see my kingdom torn apart by ambition."

He paused, his eyes flicking to Eirik, then back to the others. "There will be no fighting between you. The gods will decide."

The brothers exchanged glances, none of them willing to speak what they were all thinking. The gods had never decided anything in Norway. Blood had.

But Eirik said nothing, his hand resting on the axe at his belt, the cold steel a reminder of what would come.

In the end, it would be blood that decided. It always was.

Chapter 3
Burden of Blood

The sea churned angrily against the rocky shore, the sound of crashing waves a distant roar that echoed through the valleys. Eirik stood at the edge of the fjord, staring out at the horizon, his breath rising in the cold morning air. Behind him, the great hall of Harald Fairhair was quiet, its fires long since burned low after the previous night's revelry. He could still feel the weight of his father's words, heavy like a stone pressing down on his chest.

The gods will decide.

It was a fool's promise. The gods did not decide the fate of kings; men did. Men with axes, swords, and the will to use them. Eirik knew this better than anyone. His father might believe that peace could hold his kingdom together, but Eirik had no such illusions. Norway was a land carved from blood and iron, and it would stay that way long after Harald was gone.

He clenched his fist, feeling the cold steel of his axe in his palm. It was a small thing—little more than a hand axe—but it had served him well. The blade was sharp, well-cared for, and it had tasted blood more times than he could count. He glanced at it now, the firelight from the hall flickering in its polished edge.

His father had said there would be no fighting between the brothers, but Eirik had other plans. He would not wait for the gods to choose his fate. His brothers were not like him. They were weak, too eager for peace and honor, blind to the truth of the world. Eirik was different. He had learned the lessons of war early, and he understood that power belonged to those who were willing to take it.

"Blood is easy to spill," Harald had said.

Eirik smiled at the memory. His father was right, but he had missed the point. It was not just easy to spill—it was necessary. Without blood, there was no power, no fear, no respect. Eirik had seen the way the others looked at him, the way even his father had hesitated the night before. They feared him. And fear was power.

As the sun began to rise, painting the sky with streaks of red and gold, Eirik turned and made his way back to the hall. The day was still young, but he had work to do. The coming winter would be harsh, and the kingdom was restless. Word had already spread of his father's age and the uncertain future. Chieftains who had once bowed their heads to Harald were now whispering of rebellion, of seizing the moment to carve out their own kingdoms.

Eirik had no interest in rebellion. He wanted more than a corner of Norway. He wanted all of it.

Inside the hall, the men were beginning to stir. His brothers sat around the central hearth, nursing cups of ale and exchanging quiet words. Ragnvald was the first to notice him, his eyes narrowing as Eirik approached.

"Bloodaxe," Ragnvald said, a smirk playing on his lips. "Still brooding, are you? Thinking of which poor fool you'll cut down next?"

Eirik ignored him and sat at the edge of the hearth, the heat of the fire warming his face. He glanced at Olaf, who was poking at the flames with a long iron rod, his expression distant. Olaf had always been the quiet one, the thinker, content to let others fight his battles. Eirik respected him for that, in his own way. But respect would not save Olaf when the time came.

"I'm thinking about our father," Eirik said at last, his voice low but clear.

Ragnvald snorted. "Harald is an old man. He's had his time. The sooner we take his place, the better."

"You're a fool," Eirik said, his eyes never leaving the fire. "Our father's name still holds this kingdom together. If he falls, so does everything he's built."

"And you would be king, then?" Olaf asked quietly, not looking up from the fire. His voice was calm, but there was an edge to it, a sharpness that Eirik recognized. "You think you're the one to hold it all together?"

"I *know* I am," Eirik replied, meeting Olaf's gaze. "You, Ragnvald, the others—you're not like me. You don't have the stomach for what's coming."

"And what's coming, brother?" Ragnvald asked, leaning forward, his face hardening. "Another war? Another bloodbath? Is that what you want?"

Eirik turned to face him, his expression cold. "It's not what I want. It's what will happen. There are chieftains already plotting against us, looking for weaknesses. You think they'll wait for Father to die peacefully in his sleep? They'll strike the moment they sense any weakness."

Olaf raised an eyebrow. "And what do you propose? Kill them all before they have a chance?"

"If I have to," Eirik said simply.

Ragnvald shook his head. "You've always been a bloodthirsty bastard, Eirik, but this… this is madness."

"No," Eirik said softly. "It's survival."

The silence that followed was thick with unspoken words. Eirik could see the doubt in his brothers' eyes, the fear that was slowly creeping into their hearts. They didn't understand, not yet. But they would. When the time came, they would see that Eirik had been right all along.

He stood, the scrape of his axe against his belt the only sound in the hall. "Father's time is ending. The kingdom will not survive unless one of us is willing to do what must be done."

"And you think that's you?" Olaf asked, his voice tinged with something that might have been sadness.

"I don't think," Eirik said. "I know."

With that, he turned and left the hall, the door slamming shut behind him. Outside, the wind howled through the fjords, the first hint of winter's bite in the air. Eirik welcomed it. The cold had always been his ally, a reminder of the harshness of life, the necessity of strength.

The next few days passed in uneasy silence. Harald's sons went about their duties, but the tension between them had grown palpable. Eirik spent most of his time away from the hall, his mind consumed with thoughts of what was to come. He could feel the shift in the air, the way the winds of fate were blowing. There was a storm coming, and Eirik was ready for it.

One morning, as he sharpened his axe by the shore, a familiar voice broke the stillness.

"Eirik."

He turned to see his mother, Ragnhild, standing a few paces away. Her face was lined with age, but her eyes were still sharp, piercing him with a look that only a mother could give.

"Your father is dying," she said quietly.

Eirik nodded. "I know."

She stepped closer, her voice barely more than a whisper. "You're going to kill them, aren't you? Your brothers."

Eirik didn't answer immediately. He looked down at the blade in his hand, the edge gleaming in the morning light. Finally, he spoke.

"If I don't, they'll kill me."

Ragnhild sighed, her shoulders sagging under the weight of her son's words. She had always known that Eirik was different, even as a child. There had been a darkness in him, a hunger for power that none of her other sons possessed. But now, seeing him standing there, his axe in hand, she realized just how far that hunger had taken him.

"You're my son," she said softly, her voice trembling. "But I don't recognize you anymore."

Eirik's jaw tightened, but he didn't look at her. "You don't have to recognize me, Mother. You just have to accept that this is the way it has to be."

"And what about your father?" she asked, her voice sharp now. "What will he say when he sees what you've done?"

Eirik turned to face her, his eyes cold and unfeeling. "He'll say I did what was necessary."

Ragnhild said nothing. She simply stood there, her heart breaking for the son she had lost, the man who now stood before her in his place. Without another word, she turned and walked away, leaving Eirik alone with his thoughts.

As the wind howled once more through the fjords, Eirik gripped his axe tightly, his mind clear. There was no turning back now.

Chapter 4
Sword in the Shadows

Eirik sat at the prow of his longship as it cut through the cold waters of the fjord, the rhythmic slap of the oars the only sound breaking the morning silence. His men rowed with steady precision, their faces as grim as their leader's. They knew why they were sailing, and they knew what was coming. Eirik had gathered them quickly—hard men, warriors who had fought at his side in the distant skirmishes that now seemed like a prelude to the bloodbath ahead. They trusted him because they feared him, and that suited Eirik just fine.

The air smelled of salt and pine, sharp in the crispness of early winter. Eirik's thoughts were a storm of calculated moves and potential threats. The time for subtlety was over. His brothers might still cling to the hope of peace, but Eirik understood the truth: power came from the sharp edge of a blade, and the one who struck first held the advantage.

Father is dying, his mother's words echoed in his mind, heavy with the weight of inevitability. But Harald Fairhair was not dead yet, and that meant the kingdom still held together by a thin thread. Eirik's plan had begun to take shape long before his father's body had begun to fail him. Now, with every oar stroke that brought him closer to his destination, the pieces fell into place.

That night, as the longship glided into a small, hidden cove on the western shore, Eirik's mind was consumed by a single thought: betrayal.

He had chosen his target carefully. Of all his brothers, Hakon was the most dangerous, not because of his skill with a sword but because of his cunning. Hakon had always been the one who preferred negotiation to violence, but Eirik knew better than to mistake that for weakness. Hakon was building alliances—quietly, steadily—pulling men of influence to his side. He was preparing for the inevitable struggle for the throne, but unlike Ragnvald or Olaf, Hakon had the patience to wait, to strike when the time was right.

Eirik couldn't allow that to happen.

As his men beached the longship and began unloading their gear, Eirik slipped into the shadows, moving silently through the forest that lined the shore. His heart was steady, his breath controlled. The axe at his side felt light in his hand, a familiar weight. Ahead, in a small clearing, the glow of a campfire flickered through the trees. Hakon's men were not expecting him; they thought themselves safe this far from the hall.

That would be their mistake.

The fire crackled in the center of the camp, casting long shadows that danced across the faces of Hakon's men. There were five of them, warriors loyal to Hakon, though Eirik knew their loyalty was only as deep as their fear. He crouched low in the brush, watching them for a moment, his eyes cold and calculating.

Hakon sat apart from the others, his back to the fire, staring out into the darkness as if sensing something was coming. His long cloak hung loosely around his shoulders, and the sword at his side was sheathed. He had always been the quiet one, the thoughtful one. Even now, with the threat of death hanging over him, Hakon did not seem afraid. It was almost as if he were waiting for this.

Eirik moved swiftly. Before any of the men realized what was happening, he was upon them. His axe flashed in the firelight, the blade biting deep into the neck of the first man, who fell without a sound. The others leapt to their feet, scrambling for their weapons, but they were slow, too slow. Eirik's blade swung again, splitting the skull of a second man, the sound of bone cracking like a thunderclap in the still night air.

The third man rushed at him with a spear, but Eirik sidestepped the thrust with ease, bringing his axe down in a savage arc that severed the man's arm at the elbow. He screamed, falling to the ground, clutching the bloody stump as his lifeblood soaked the earth.

Hakon's voice cut through the chaos, calm and steady. "Enough."

Eirik turned, breathing hard, his axe dripping with blood. Hakon had not drawn his sword. He stood at the edge of the firelight, watching the slaughter with an expression that was neither fear nor anger. There was only resignation.

"You've come for my head, then," Hakon said quietly.

Eirik wiped the blood from his axe on his cloak, his eyes never leaving his brother's face. "You would have come for mine, eventually."

Hakon smiled faintly, though there was no warmth in it. "Perhaps. But not like this. Not in the dark, like a thief."

"I'm no thief," Eirik said, his voice cold. "I'm taking what's mine."

Hakon's eyes flickered to the bodies of his men, lying in twisted heaps around the fire. "Is this how you plan to rule? Through blood and fear? Father's kingdom will not last if you tear it apart."

"Father's kingdom *already* lies in pieces," Eirik snarled, stepping closer. "He just doesn't know it yet."

Hakon's gaze hardened. "And what do you think will happen when he finds out? When he sees what you've done?"

"I don't care what he thinks," Eirik said. "He's dying. His time is over."

For a moment, Hakon said nothing. He stood there, the firelight casting shadows across his face, his hand resting on the hilt of his sword but making no move to draw it. Finally, he sighed, as if letting go of something he had held onto for too long.

"Then do it," Hakon said quietly. "Kill me. End this."

Eirik hesitated, just for a second. Hakon had always been different from the others. He was not like Ragnvald, who boasted and blustered, or Olaf, who schemed and manipulated. Hakon had always seemed to know something the rest of them didn't, something deeper, something darker.

But that didn't matter now.

Eirik raised his axe.

The next morning, Eirik and his men stood over the blood-soaked camp. The sun was just beginning to rise, painting the sky with streaks of pale blue and gold. Hakon's body lay where it had fallen, his blood mingling with the ashes of the fire.

Eirik stared down at his brother's lifeless form, his heart as cold as the steel in his hand. He felt no triumph, no satisfaction. This had been necessary—nothing more, nothing less. Hakon had been a threat, and now he was gone. But there would be more threats, more blood to spill before Eirik could claim what was rightfully his.

The wind stirred the trees around them, carrying the scent of salt and death. Eirik turned to his men, his voice calm but firm.

"Burn the bodies," he said. "We leave no trace."

As his warriors moved to carry out his orders, Eirik stood alone at the edge of the camp, his eyes on the horizon. He could feel the weight of what was to come pressing down on him, heavy and unrelenting. This was only the beginning.

The blood would flow, and Eirik would be at its center.

But as he watched the flames rise, devouring the remains of his brother and his men, a dark thought crept into his mind. His father still lived. And while Harald drew breath, Eirik's claim to the throne was uncertain.

He had removed one rival. But the greatest obstacle still remained.

Harald Fairhair would die. Eirik would make sure of it.

Chapter 5
The King's Shadow

The heavy oak doors of Harald Fairhair's hall groaned as they swung open, and Eirik stepped inside, his boots echoing off the stone floor. It was cold in the great hall, colder than Eirik remembered, as if the life of the kingdom itself was withering away with his father. The hearth fires flickered weakly, their light barely cutting through the gloom. The familiar scent of smoke, mead, and damp wood filled the air, but there was something else now—a smell of decay, faint but unmistakable.

Harald Fairhair sat on his high seat at the far end of the hall, his once-powerful frame shrunken by age. His hair, once golden and thick, had turned to wisps of white, his face gaunt and hollow. Yet his eyes were still sharp, still watching every movement, every breath. He was no longer the mighty warrior who had united Norway through blood and iron, but the presence of a king still clung to him, like a mantle too heavy for his frail shoulders.

Eirik walked forward, every step measured, controlled. He could feel the eyes of the other men in the hall, watching him from the shadows. Chieftains, jarls, men who had once fought alongside his father, now wondering what would become of them once the old king was gone. They all knew what Eirik had done—word had spread faster than the winter winds. Hakon was dead, and with him, one of the last pillars of resistance. But they didn't know the whole truth. Not yet.

As Eirik reached the foot of his father's seat, he paused, lowering his head in a show of respect. "Father."

Harald's voice was a rasp, like the sound of dead leaves rustling in the wind. "So, it's true then. Hakon is gone."

Eirik nodded, keeping his face impassive. "He was planning to betray you. I did what had to be done."

The old king's eyes narrowed. "Did he, now? Or was it you who betrayed him?"

A flicker of irritation passed through Eirik, but he kept his voice steady. "He was building alliances,

Father. He would have taken the throne the moment you were gone."

Harald's laugh was a brittle, hollow thing, like a bone snapping underfoot. "Do you think I'm blind, boy? I know what my sons have been plotting. All of you, grasping at what's mine before I'm even cold in the ground."

Eirik stiffened, the muscles in his jaw tightening. "I've been loyal to you. I've done what you couldn't."

Harald leaned forward, his eyes burning with a sudden intensity. "Loyal? Is that what you call it? Killing your brothers, tearing this kingdom apart from within? You think this is what I wanted when I carved out Norway from the hands of our enemies?"

Eirik met his father's gaze, his voice low and unyielding. "This is the only way to hold it together. The others are weak. They would let everything you built crumble to dust."

"And you think you're strong enough to hold it all, do you?" Harald asked, his voice dripping with contempt. "You think you're fit to be king?"

Eirik said nothing, but his silence spoke louder than any words. He could feel the tension in the room rising, the air thick with unspoken threats. The other men shifted uneasily in their seats, their eyes darting between father and son. This was no longer just a conversation. This was a reckoning.

Harald's face twisted into something that might have been a smile, though there was no warmth in it. "You may have killed Hakon, but you'll find that ruling is a different kind of battle. You can't hack through a kingdom with an axe, no matter how sharp it is."

"I don't intend to," Eirik replied, his voice steady. "But I will do what's necessary."

The old king's gaze lingered on him for a long moment, and then, with a weary sigh, he leaned back in his chair, as if the weight of his crown had finally become too much to bear. "Do you think I don't know what you're planning, boy? You want my throne. You always have."

Eirik didn't deny it. There was no point in pretending otherwise. "Your time is over, Father. The kingdom needs someone strong, someone willing to do what you can't."

Harald's eyes flickered with a mixture of anger and sorrow. "You think you're strong because you've killed a few men? You think you can hold this kingdom together with blood and fear? You're a fool, Eirik. A fool blinded by ambition."

Eirik felt his fists clench at his sides, the anger bubbling just beneath the surface. "And what would you have me do, Father? Sit by and watch as our enemies tear us apart? Let my brothers scheme and plot until they're ready to stab me in the back? I'm not like you. I won't let anyone take what's mine."

Harald's voice was suddenly soft, almost a whisper. "You think the throne is yours, but you're wrong. The throne belongs to the people. It always has. Without them, you're nothing."

Eirik sneered. "The people will follow whoever has the strength to lead. And I'm the only one left who has that strength."

The old king closed his eyes, a deep sadness settling over him like a shroud. "You'll learn soon enough, boy. The burden of kingship is not just in the wielding of power. It's in the choices you make, the lives you destroy."

Eirik's jaw tightened. "I'm not afraid of hard choices."

Harald opened his eyes again, fixing his son with a stare that seemed to pierce straight through him. "Then you're already lost."

That night, the hall was eerily quiet, the tension hanging in the air like a suffocating mist. The chieftains had withdrawn to their quarters, their whispers fading into the darkness as they discussed what would come next. Harald Fairhair was dying, and the vultures were circling.

Eirik sat alone by the hearth, staring into the flames. His father's words gnawed at him, a persistent whisper in the back of his mind. He had always known that taking the throne would require sacrifice—blood had to be spilled, alliances broken, trust shattered. That was the way of kings. But there had been something in Harald's eyes, something that Eirik couldn't shake.

The throne belongs to the people.

What did that even mean? The people were sheep, easily led, easily frightened. They would follow whoever had the strength to seize the crown and hold it. That was the way of things. His father's talk of burdens and choices sounded like the ramblings of a man too old to remember the realities of power.

But then why did it still bother him?

The fire crackled, and Eirik's hand tightened around the hilt of his axe. He had come too far to turn back now. He had killed his brothers, secured his alliances, and positioned himself as the strongest of

Harald's sons. There was no room for doubt, no space for weakness.

And yet, in the stillness of the night, as the flames flickered and danced, a shadow seemed to fall over him—a shadow cast by the dying king in the high seat, a shadow that would linger long after the fires burned out.

At dawn, Eirik stood by the shore, watching the sun rise over the fjords. The cold wind bit at his face, but he barely noticed. His mind was elsewhere, consumed by the path ahead. His father would not last much longer, and when he was gone, the kingdom would be Eirik's to claim. But it wouldn't be easy. Even with Hakon dead, there were still others who would challenge him—men who would not bend the knee so easily.

As the waves lapped against the rocks, a figure approached from the shadows, moving with the grace of a seasoned warrior. Eirik turned, recognizing the man immediately—Skarde, his most trusted lieutenant. The man's face was hard, scarred from years of battle, but there was a glint in his eye that told Eirik he had news.

"It's done," Skarde said quietly, his voice barely more than a whisper.

Eirik nodded, his expression unreadable. "Good. And the others?"

"They're waiting for your signal. When the old man dies, we'll move quickly."

Eirik looked out at the horizon, his heart a cold, heavy weight in his chest. He had come this far. There was no turning back now.

"When my father dies," Eirik said, his voice as cold as the wind, "I'll take the throne."

Skarde hesitated, glancing at Eirik with a flicker of doubt. "And if the people resist?"

Eirik's eyes darkened, the shadow of his father's words still lingering. "Then we'll show them what happens to those who resist the will of a king."

The wind howled through the fjords, a warning of the storm to come.

Chapter 6
A King's Final Words

The great hall of Harald Fairhair was silent as the grave. The once-vibrant tapestries that adorned the walls now seemed faded and distant, their colors muted by the gloom of impending death. Harald sat in his high seat, the weight of his years and the burden of his imminent passing etched deeply into his face. The last embers of the hearth glowed weakly, casting long shadows that stretched across the hall like fingers reaching into the past.

Eirik stood before his father, his posture straight and his expression carefully controlled. He had come to pay his respects—or so it appeared. In reality, he was waiting, watching, ready for the moment when the old king would take his final breath and the kingdom would be his.

Harald's breathing was labored, each inhale a struggle, each exhale a reminder of the end that was drawing near. His eyes, once sharp and commanding, were now clouded with a mixture of pain and resignation. Eirik could see the flicker of life slowly fading, and he felt a pang of something—perhaps regret, perhaps anticipation. The end was close, and with it, his chance to seize the throne.

A hush fell over the hall as the elder chieftains and advisors gathered, their faces a mix of solemnity and anxiety. They knew what was coming, and they were waiting to see who would emerge as the new leader. Eirik's presence was a deliberate choice—he was making a statement, positioning himself as the natural successor, the one who would carry on his father's legacy.

Harald's gaze shifted slowly, meeting Eirik's eyes. For a moment, there was something in that gaze—a flicker of recognition, a hint of the old king's strength. Then, with a final effort, Harald raised his trembling hand, signaling for his sons to come closer.

"Eirik," he rasped, his voice barely more than a whisper. "Come closer."

Eirik stepped forward, his heart pounding in his chest. The moment was drawing near, and he had to be ready. The eyes of the assembly were upon him, their expectation a heavy weight on his shoulders. He could feel the tension in the air, thick and palpable, as if the very hall was holding its breath.

Harald's hand reached out, gripping Eirik's arm with a surprising strength. "You think you're ready to be king," he said, his voice cracking with the effort. "But being a king is more than just taking a throne. It's about leading with wisdom, with justice."

Eirik nodded, his expression impassive. "I understand, Father."

"Do you?" Harald's eyes bore into him, intense and piercing despite the failing light. "You think you can rule with fear alone, but that will not hold a kingdom together. People need more than just a strong hand. They need a vision, a hope."

"I'll give them that," Eirik said firmly. "I'll be a strong ruler."

Harald's gaze softened, a touch of sadness mingling with the pain. "A king who rules by fear may keep his throne, but he will never have the love or loyalty of his people. They will follow you as long as you can control them, but the moment you falter, they will turn against you."

Eirik's jaw tightened. He had heard these words before, from his father and others. They spoke of loyalty and love, but Eirik knew that power was what truly mattered. Power was what held the kingdom together.

"You should have thought of that before you began plotting against me," Eirik said quietly, though there was no malice in his tone. "It's too late for regrets now."

Harald's grip on his arm loosened, his eyes growing dim. "The kingdom… my kingdom… will need more than just a strong hand. It will need a leader who understands the balance between power and compassion."

Eirik felt a pang of irritation at the old king's words. They were not what he wanted to hear. He had already made his decision, and nothing would change his mind now.

"I'll do what needs to be done," Eirik said, his voice steely and resolute. "You don't have to worry about that."

Harald's eyes closed, his breathing growing more labored. The room fell into a tense silence, the anticipation of the end hanging heavy in the air. The old king's final moments were a grim reminder of the reality of power—the way it could slip through one's fingers, even when it seemed secure.

As the final breath left Harald's lips, Eirik stood over him, his expression a mask of stoic resolve. The old king was gone, and with him, the last vestiges of a unified Norway. Eirik's path was clear, and the way to the throne lay open before him.

The hall erupted into a murmur of shock and grief as the reality of Harald's death settled over the assembly. Eirik could see the uncertainty in the faces of the chieftains and advisors, the fear of what was to come. They were looking to him now, waiting to see how he would handle the transition.

Eirik stepped back from the body, taking a deep breath as he prepared to address the assembly. He needed to show strength, to assert his dominance in a way that would leave no room for doubt.

"My father is dead," Eirik's voice rang out, clear and commanding. "The throne is mine by right. I will lead this kingdom into a new era, one of strength and prosperity. Those who oppose me will face the consequences."

The room fell silent again, the weight of Eirik's words settling over the assembly. The chieftains exchanged uneasy glances, their loyalty now in question. Eirik could see the shift in the room—the way the dynamics were changing, the way some of the men were already beginning to align themselves with the new ruler.

The path to the throne was not yet fully secured, but Eirik knew that he had made the first crucial step. He had taken control of the moment, seized the opportunity, and now it was time to solidify his position.

As he stood before the assembly, Eirik could feel the eyes of his father's legacy weighing heavily upon him. The old king's final words still echoed in his mind, a reminder of the challenge that lay ahead. To be a king was more than just holding the throne—it was about commanding respect, inspiring loyalty, and maintaining control.

Eirik's heart was cold, his mind focused on the path ahead. The kingdom was his to shape, and he would do so with the strength and determination that had brought him this far.

But even as he prepared to claim his victory, a shadow lingered over him—a reminder that the road to power was never straightforward, and the legacy of Harald Fairhair would not be so easily cast aside.

Chapter 7
Gathering Storm

The days following Harald Fairhair's death were marked by a flurry of activity, as chieftains and advisors from across the kingdom converged on the great hall to witness the transition of power. The air was thick with tension and uncertainty, as each man sought to secure his place in the new order. Eirik Bloodaxe had taken the throne, but the crown was not yet firmly in his grasp.

In the bustling city of Nidaros, the center of the kingdom, the preparations for the coronation were underway. Eirik had moved quickly to solidify his claim, but not without resistance. The chieftains were reluctant to pledge their loyalty without assurances of their own power and influence in the new regime. The old alliances were shifting, and Eirik had to navigate the treacherous waters of politics with the same skill he had used in battle.

Eirik stood in the courtyard of the great hall, watching as his men prepared for the upcoming ceremony. The sun was setting, casting long shadows across the stone walls. The courtyard was alive with activity—servants and warriors moving in a coordinated frenzy, setting up the ceremonial space with tapestries and banners, preparing the feast that would follow the coronation. Eirik's trusted lieutenant, Skarde, stood beside him, his expression as grim as ever.

"It's almost time," Skarde said, his voice low. "The chieftains are gathering, and the word is spreading quickly. Some are eager to pledge their loyalty, but others are still waiting to see how the wind blows."

Eirik nodded, his gaze fixed on the preparations. "I expected as much. We'll need to show strength and decisiveness. If we let any sign of weakness show, we'll face challenges we can't afford."

Skarde glanced at Eirik, his eyes reflecting a flicker of concern. "And what about those who remain neutral or even hostile? There are whispers of rebellion and unrest in the southern parts of the kingdom. Some are saying that Hakon's death was but the beginning."

Eirik's jaw tightened. "We'll deal with any dissent swiftly. There can be no tolerance for those who would undermine my rule. I intend to make an example of anyone who dares to oppose me."

Skarde nodded, though there was a hint of unease in his expression. "And what of the other brothers? Ragnvald and Olaf?"

"They will be dealt with in time," Eirik replied tersely. "For now, our focus must be on securing the support of the chieftains and quelling any immediate threats. Once we have established our dominance, we can turn our attention to the others."

The sound of horns announcing the arrival of the chieftains interrupted their conversation. Eirik turned to see a procession of men in rich furs and fine robes making their way into the courtyard. Each one carried the insignia of his clan, a symbol of his authority and power. They moved with a mixture of awe and apprehension, their eyes fixed on the man who would soon be crowned king.

Eirik took a deep breath, steadying himself for the task ahead. He had fought hard for this moment, and now it was time to seize it fully. As the chieftains took their places, Eirik walked to the center of the courtyard, his presence commanding immediate attention. The crowd fell silent, the weight of expectation hanging heavily in the air.

The chief priest of the kingdom stepped forward, his robes flowing around him like a sea of white. He raised his hands, invoking the gods and calling for their blessing on the new king. Eirik stood tall, his gaze unwavering as the ceremonial rites began.

The priest's voice intoned the ancient words, the language of the gods reverberating through the courtyard.

Eirik's thoughts were focused on the future, on the challenges that lay ahead. The coronation was a crucial step, but it was only the beginning. The kingdom was fraught with division and unrest, and Eirik knew that securing his rule would require more than just symbolic gestures. He would need to demonstrate his strength and cunning, to show that he was not just a king by right, but a ruler who could command respect and loyalty.

As the ceremony progressed, Eirik felt a sense of resolve building within him. The crown was placed upon his head, a weight both literal and metaphorical. He accepted it with a mixture of pride and determination, aware of the immense responsibility that came with it.

The crowd erupted in cheers as Eirik was proclaimed king, the sound of their approval mingling with the clash of swords and the rhythm of drums. It was a moment of triumph, but Eirik knew better than to let his guard down. The true test of his reign would come in the days and weeks to follow, as he navigated the complexities of ruling a kingdom in flux.

As the celebrations continued into the night, Eirik retired to his chambers, his mind a whirlwind of thoughts and plans. The walls of his new quarters were adorned with tapestries and trophies from his victories, a testament to his prowess as a warrior. But now, as king, he would need to rely on more than just brute force. He would need to outwit his enemies, navigate the treacherous political landscape, and secure his rule through both fear and diplomacy.

Eirik sat by the window, looking out at the city of Nidaros. The streets were alive with the sounds of celebration, but Eirik's thoughts were focused on the challenges that lay ahead. The kingdom was his, but maintaining control would require careful maneuvering and relentless determination.

As he prepared for the days to come, Eirik knew that the real test of his reign was yet to begin. The gathering storm was on the horizon, and he would need to face it head-on if he was to secure his place as the true ruler of Norway.

Chapter 8
Clash of Iron

The morning mist clung to the hills around Nidaros as the sun struggled to pierce through, casting a dim, ethereal light over the land. Eirik Bloodaxe stood on a rise overlooking the valley below, the chill in the air biting at his skin. His gaze was fixed on the horizon, where dark clouds gathered ominously, a fitting prelude to the battle that was about to unfold. His kingdom, newly claimed, faced its first serious challenge—a rebellion led by a faction of discontented chieftains who refused to accept Eirik's rule.

The rebellion had been brewing for months, fueled by whispers of dissent and the discontent of those who felt left out of Eirik's new order. Among the leaders of this rebellion were several prominent chieftains and disillusioned warriors who had once been loyal to Harald Fairhair but now saw an opportunity to reclaim power for themselves. Their forces had gathered in the hills, preparing for an assault on Nidaros, determined to challenge Eirik's claim to the throne.

The camp was abuzz with activity as Eirik's men prepared for the impending clash. The clatter of armor and the murmur of anxious voices filled the air. Eirik moved among his troops, his presence a beacon of authority. His sharp eyes scanned the faces of his warriors, each one a reflection of the loyalty and resolve that would be crucial in the battle to come. He could see the apprehension in their eyes, but he also saw the fire of determination.

"Skarde," Eirik called, his voice cutting through the noise of the camp. His lieutenant approached, his expression grim but focused.

"The enemy forces are gathering in the valley," Skarde reported. "They're well-equipped and ready for a fight. We estimate their numbers to be about equal to ours, maybe a little more."

Eirik nodded, his mind already racing through the strategies and tactics that would give him the upper hand. "We need to make the first move. We can't afford to let them consolidate their position. Prepare the men for a dawn assault. We'll hit them before they have a chance to fully deploy."

Skarde's eyes narrowed in determination. "I'll see to it."

As the night descended, Eirik made his final preparations. His armor was polished and gleaming, his sword sharp and ready. The moonlight cast eerie shadows over the camp, and the silence was heavy with the anticipation of the battle to come. Eirik's mind was a whirlwind of thoughts—tactics, strategies, and the weight of leadership.

The first light of dawn broke over the horizon, and with it came the clash of steel and the roar of battle. Eirik's forces, divided into carefully planned units, advanced through the misty valley. The ground was uneven, with rocky outcrops and scattered boulders providing both cover and obstacles. Eirik's troops moved with precision, their formations tight and disciplined.

As they approached the enemy camp, the rebels, caught off guard by the sudden assault, scrambled to form a defense. The clash of iron and the cries of men filled the air as the two armies collided. Eirik fought at the forefront, his axe swinging with deadly efficiency as he carved a path through the enemy ranks. The battle was fierce, with the air filled with the stench of sweat, blood, and fear.

Eirik's strategy was clear—to break the enemy's lines and disrupt their formations. His men fought with a ferocity that matched his own, their discipline and training evident in every strike. The rebels, though numerous, were disorganized and struggling to respond to the sudden and brutal assault.

Amid the chaos, Eirik's eyes locked onto a familiar figure—the leader of the rebellion, a burly chieftain named Kjell, who had once been a trusted ally of Harald Fairhair. Kjell fought with a desperate intensity, his axe swinging wildly as he sought to turn the tide of the battle. Eirik made his way toward him, cutting through the enemy ranks with a single-minded focus.

The two men finally faced each other, their eyes locked in a fierce, unspoken challenge. Kjell's face was twisted with anger and defiance, while Eirik's expression was one of cold determination.

"You think you can take what's mine?" Kjell roared, his voice hoarse from the exertion of battle.

Eirik's eyes were steely as he replied, "You made a mistake challenging me. Now you'll pay the price."

With a ferocious battle cry, the two men clashed, their axes meeting with a resounding clang. The force of the impact reverberated through their arms, and they circled each other, each looking for an opening. Kjell was a formidable opponent, his strikes powerful and precise. But Eirik was relentless, his movements calculated and deadly.

The battle around them raged on, but for a moment, it was as if the world had narrowed to just the two of them. Eirik could feel the weight of the battle, the lives of his men depending on his victory.

He pushed forward with a surge of strength, his axe finding its mark with a brutal efficiency. Kjell staggered back, bloodied and exhausted, but he was not finished yet.

The fight continued, each blow exchanged with a grim determination. Eirik's superior technique and relentless aggression began to wear down Kjell's defenses. With a final, decisive strike, Eirik's axe crashed down, and Kjell fell to the ground, defeated and broken.

As Kjell lay sprawled on the ground, Eirik stood over him, breathing heavily but unyielding. The battle had turned in his favor, and the rebels, seeing their leader fall, began to break and flee. Eirik's men pressed their advantage, driving the remaining enemies from the field.

The battlefield was littered with the fallen, the once-vibrant landscape now a grim testament to the violence of war. Eirik surveyed the scene with a mixture of satisfaction and grim resolve. The battle was won, but the cost was high. The dead and wounded lay scattered across the ground, a stark reminder of the price of power.

As the sun climbed higher in the sky, Eirik's men began to gather, their cheers and cries a testament to their victory. Eirik stood at the center of the battlefield, his gaze sweeping over the scene. The rebellion had been crushed, but the real challenge lay ahead—securing his rule and ensuring that no other challengers would rise against him.

The road to the throne was fraught with peril, and Eirik knew that the struggle was far from over. But for now, he had proven his strength and established his dominance. The battle had been fierce, but it had also been a necessary step in solidifying his power.

As he made his way back to the camp, Eirik's thoughts were already focused on the next phase of his rule.

Chapter 9
Gathering of Allies

The aftermath of the battle left Nidaros in a state of somber triumph. The city was alive with activity as Eirik Bloodaxe's men worked to tend to the wounded, bury the dead, and secure the surrounding area. The victory had come at a high cost, and Eirik knew that the kingdom's stability depended on more than just military might. He needed to consolidate his power, forge new alliances, and ensure that his rule was accepted by those who had once opposed him.

Days after the battle, Eirik summoned the surviving chieftains and influential figures from across the realm to a great council. The meeting was to be held in the great hall of Nidaros, a symbol of both victory and the beginning of a new era. The hall, once the site of a triumphant coronation, now had a more somber atmosphere as it prepared to host a crucial gathering that would shape the future of Norway.

The chieftains arrived in a steady stream, their retinues and entourages making their way through the city's bustling streets. They came with a mix of apprehension and curiosity, eager to see how Eirik would address the recent conflict and what promises he might offer in exchange for their support. The hall was filled with the murmur of voices and the clinking of metal as the chieftains settled into their places, their eyes fixed on the throne at the head of the room.

Eirik stood before them, his posture confident and his expression commanding. The battle had strengthened his resolve, and he was determined to use this council to solidify his position and address the grievances of those who had opposed him. Skarde, his loyal lieutenant, stood by his side, ready to assist in any way necessary.

As the final chieftains took their seats, Eirik raised his hand, signaling for silence. The room gradually quieted, the weight of expectation hanging heavily in the air.

"Loyal chieftains," Eirik began, his voice carrying a tone of authority. "You have all witnessed the cost of our recent conflict. The battle was fierce, but it was necessary to secure our future. We must now look forward and work together to rebuild and strengthen our kingdom."

He paused, allowing his words to sink in. The chieftains listened intently, their expressions a mix of skepticism and hope. Eirik knew that gaining their trust would require more than just promises—it would require tangible actions and concessions.

"I recognize that many of you have suffered losses," Eirik continued. "The bloodshed was not something I desired, but it was a necessity to eliminate those who sought to undermine our unity. Now, we must turn our efforts toward healing the divisions and ensuring that our kingdom stands strong."

A murmur of agreement rippled through the room, and Eirik seized the moment to make his next move. "To this end, I am prepared to offer a series of concessions and agreements. I will grant land and titles to those who have supported me and will work to address the grievances of those who have been wronged."

One of the chieftains, a grizzled warrior named Torvald, rose from his seat. "And what of the lands and people that were taken in the conflict? How will you ensure that justice is done for those who have been wronged?"

Eirik met Torvald's gaze, his expression resolute. "I will appoint a council of trusted advisors to oversee the redistribution of land and resources. We will ensure that those who have been affected by the conflict receive fair compensation and that justice is served."

Torvald nodded, though his expression remained guarded. "And what of those who still harbor ill will towards you? How will you deal with them?"

Eirik's eyes hardened. "Those who remain a threat to the kingdom's stability will be dealt with swiftly and decisively. However, I am open to negotiations and am willing to offer amnesty to those who are willing to swear loyalty and contribute to the kingdom's future."

The room was filled with a tense silence as the chieftains exchanged glances. Eirik's offer of amnesty and concessions was a significant gesture, but it was clear that many of them remained wary. The battle had not only been a clash of armies but a struggle for control and influence, and gaining the trust of these leaders would be a delicate and ongoing process.

As the council continued, Eirik outlined his plans for the kingdom's reconstruction and future governance. He spoke of new trade agreements, improved infrastructure, and measures to strengthen the kingdom's defenses. Each promise was carefully calculated to address the needs and concerns of the chieftains and to demonstrate his commitment to a unified and prosperous Norway.

Despite the progress, there were still dissenting voices and simmering tensions. Eirik knew that his rule was far from secure and that the path ahead would be fraught with challenges. The council was just the beginning of a long and arduous process of consolidation and diplomacy.

As the meeting concluded, Eirik felt a mix of relief and apprehension. The council had been a step toward stability, but the true test would come in the months and years ahead. He needed to navigate the complex web of alliances and rivalries, to prove that he was more than just a victorious warrior but a capable and just ruler.

The chieftains departed, each one taking with them their own hopes and doubts. Eirik watched them leave, his mind already turning to the next phase of his rule. The kingdom was his to shape, but the road ahead would require careful negotiation, strategic alliances, and unwavering determination.

As the great hall emptied and the echoes of the council faded, Eirik turned to Skarde. "We've made progress, but there's still much to be done. We need to remain vigilant and continue to build our alliances. The future of Norway depends on it."

Skarde nodded in agreement. "We'll see to it. The challenges are far from over, but we're ready to face them."

Eirik looked out over the city of Nidaros, his gaze steady and unyielding. The path to securing his rule was a long and treacherous one, but he was determined to see it through. The kingdom of Norway was at a crossroads.

Chapter 10
Iron Web

As autumn's chill settled over Norway, Eirik Bloodaxe's victory was both recent and tenuous. The newly crowned king faced the daunting task of solidifying his rule amidst the fractured loyalties and simmering unrest that lingered in the wake of the recent rebellion. His enemies had been subdued, but the threat of further dissent loomed large. Eirik knew that to secure his throne, he needed to consolidate power, address grievances, and, most critically, eliminate any remaining threats to his authority.

The city of Nidaros had begun to recover from the recent upheavals. The streets, once echoing with the sounds of battle, were now filled with the hustle of reconstruction and the murmur of new rumors. Eirik's men had worked tirelessly to repair the damage caused by the conflict, and the once somber mood of the city was slowly being replaced by an uneasy sense of normalcy.

Eirik, however, remained focused on his broader strategy. He convened a private meeting with his trusted advisors in the dimly lit war room of the royal palace. The room, decorated with maps and battle standards, was a stark contrast to the grand and often chaotic council chamber. Here, Eirik and his closest confidants could speak candidly about the issues at hand.

Skarde stood by the large oak table, his expression as grim as ever. "The rebellion has left its mark, and though we've made strides, we still face significant challenges. The southern regions are particularly restless. Some of the chieftains who pledged allegiance to you are wavering, and there are whispers of another uprising."

Eirik's eyes narrowed as he studied the map spread before him. "We must act decisively. I want to know who among our allies might be plotting against us. I need a list of all the chieftains who have shown any signs of dissent or hesitation. We'll make an example of them if necessary."

The room was silent, the weight of Eirik's command hanging heavily in the air. His advisors exchanged uneasy glances but nodded in understanding. Eirik's reputation for ruthlessness was well-known, and it was clear that he intended to use it to maintain control.

"Our spies have reported suspicious activity in the south," Skarde continued. "One of the chieftains, Jarl Haldor, has been particularly active. He's known for his ambition and has been seen meeting with discontented factions. It's possible he's trying to stir up trouble."

Eirik's gaze was cold and calculating. "Haldor's ambition will be his downfall. Send word to him that he is to appear at court within the week. If he refuses, we'll have to take more drastic measures."

Skarde nodded, and the meeting continued with discussions on the distribution of resources, the strengthening of fortifications, and the management of the kingdom's finances. Eirik's plans were meticulous, aimed at securing every aspect of his rule. He knew that a single misstep could unravel everything he had worked for.

As night fell, Eirik retired to his chambers, his mind still buzzing with plans and strategies. His wife, Queen Gunnhild, entered the room, her face reflecting the strains of recent events. She approached him with a concerned expression.

"Eirik, the tension in the court is palpable," she said softly. "Many are afraid of what might happen next. They're loyal to you, but they're also fearful of your methods."

Eirik looked at her with a mixture of irritation and resolve. "Fear is a tool, Gunnhild. It keeps people in line. They will learn that opposing me comes with a heavy price. It is the only way to ensure stability."

Gunnhild's eyes softened, though she remained troubled. "I understand your need for control, but you must also be wary of alienating those who could be valuable allies. Diplomacy and trust can be just as powerful as fear."

Eirik's expression hardened. "Trust is earned, not given. I will not risk my rule on the hope that others will remain loyal simply because they like me. I will use every means at my disposal to secure my position."

With that, Eirik turned his attention back to his maps and documents, signaling the end of their conversation. Gunnhild left the room, her concern evident, but Eirik remained focused on his plans.

The next morning, Eirik's emissaries delivered summonses to Jarl Haldor and other key figures suspected of dissent. The invitations were met with mixed reactions. Some chieftains were eager to comply, while others viewed the summons with suspicion and fear.

As the day of Haldor's appearance approached, Eirik's court was a hive of activity. The great hall was prepared for a formal audience, with elaborate tapestries and banners displaying Eirik's newly asserted authority. The air was thick with anticipation and unease as the chieftains gathered.

Haldor arrived at the court with a sizable retinue, his demeanor defiant but cautious. He entered the hall with a sense of pride, though it was evident that he was wary of the king's intentions. Eirik greeted him with a cold smile as he took his place on the throne, flanked by his advisors and guards.

"Jarl Haldor," Eirik began, his voice carrying an edge of authority. "I trust you've received my summons. You know the purpose of this audience?"

Haldor bowed slightly, his face a mask of composure. "Yes, my king. I am here to address any concerns you may have."

Eirik's eyes narrowed. "There have been reports of your involvement with factions opposed to my rule. I want to know the truth of these claims. Are you conspiring against me?"

Haldor's expression remained neutral, though a flicker of unease passed through his eyes. "My loyalty to the king is unwavering. If there have been misunderstandings, I am here to clear them up."

Eirik leaned forward, his gaze piercing. "Misunderstandings? Or are you testing the waters for your own ambitions?"

Haldor's composure faltered slightly, but he quickly regained his footing. "My ambitions are for the betterment of the kingdom, not for personal gain. If there are grievances, I am open to addressing them."

Eirik's eyes were cold as he assessed Haldor's response. "Very well. I will give you the opportunity to prove your loyalty. However, know that any further evidence of disloyalty will be met with severe consequences."

The audience continued with discussions about the kingdom's governance and the role of the chieftains in maintaining stability. Haldor was forced to pledge his loyalty and agree to Eirik's conditions, but the tension in the room was palpable.

As the court adjourned, Eirik's mind was already focused on his next steps. The meeting with Haldor had been a necessary part of his strategy, but he knew that the true challenge lay in maintaining control and preventing further dissent. The kingdom was his to rule, but the web of intrigue and ambition was ever-present, threatening to unravel his carefully laid plans.

Eirik's thoughts turned to the broader strategy for dealing with the remaining dissenters and solidifying his rule. The battle was won, but the real work of maintaining power and ensuring the kingdom's stability had only just begun. The Iron

Web of alliances and rivalries was complex and treacherous, and Eirik was determined to navigate it with the same ruthlessness and cunning that had brought him to the throne.

As he looked out over the city of Nidaros, Eirik felt a sense of grim satisfaction. The kingdom was his to shape, and he would use every tool at his disposal to secure his place as the ruler of Norway.

Chapter 11
Betrayal

The cold winds of late autumn swept through Nidaros, carrying with them whispers of unrest and betrayal. The city, still recovering from the recent battles, was alive with rumors and suspicions. Eirik Bloodaxe, ever vigilant and calculating, had been keenly aware of the shifting dynamics among the chieftains and their factions. He knew that in the game of power, even the slightest hint of discontent could unravel his hard-won rule.

Eirik's focus had shifted to a new threat, one that had emerged from within his own ranks. The loyalty of his trusted allies was now in question, and the shadows of treachery loomed large. His spies had reported troubling signs of dissent among some of his own men, and whispers of a conspiracy had begun to circulate.

The great hall of Nidaros, once a symbol of Eirik's power and authority, had become a place of tension and scrutiny. Eirik had called a private meeting with his most trusted advisors and loyal followers to address the growing concerns. The room was dimly lit by flickering torches, casting long shadows on the stone walls. Eirik sat at the head of the table, his expression one of cold determination.

Skarde, his ever-reliable lieutenant, stood beside him, a grim look on his face. "My lord," Skarde began, "the reports from our spies have become increasingly concerning. There are indications that some of your closest advisors may be involved in plotting against you. We have evidence suggesting that a faction within your court is working to undermine your authority."

Eirik's eyes narrowed, his mind already racing through the possibilities. "Who are these traitors? And what evidence do we have of their involvement?"

Skarde spread out a series of documents and reports on the table. "These are intercepted messages and accounts from our informants. The key figures in question are Jarl Erik, one of your trusted allies, and Thord, a high-ranking officer in your guard. They have been seen meeting with known dissenters and discussing plans that could destabilize your rule."

Eirik's jaw tightened as he scanned the documents. Jarl Erik had been one of the first to pledge allegiance to him after the death of Harald Fairhair, and Thord was a veteran warrior whose loyalty had once seemed unshakable. The thought of betrayal from such trusted individuals was both infuriating and troubling.

"This treachery will not go unpunished," Eirik said, his voice cold and steely. "We must act swiftly to uncover the full extent of this conspiracy and deal with it before it grows."

Skarde nodded in agreement. "I will initiate a discreet investigation to gather more evidence and determine the full scope of the betrayal. We should also consider preemptive measures to neutralize any threats before they can take action."

Eirik leaned back in his chair, his mind working through the implications of the betrayal. The very fabric of his power was at stake, and he knew that any sign of weakness would be exploited by his enemies. He needed to act with both precision and ruthlessness.

"Send for Jarl Erik and Thord," Eirik ordered. "We will confront them directly. If they are innocent, they will have nothing to fear. But if they are guilty, they will face the consequences of their betrayal."

As the day wore on, Jarl Erik and Thord were summoned to the palace. The atmosphere in the great hall was charged with tension as the two men arrived, their expressions a mixture of apprehension and defiance. They were ushered into the hall where Eirik awaited them, his demeanor as cold as the northern winds.

Jarl Erik, a tall and imposing figure, met Eirik's gaze with a steady look. "My king," he said, his voice betraying no hint of nervousness. "You summoned me. What is the purpose of this meeting?"

Eirik's eyes were sharp and unforgiving. "You are accused of conspiring against me. Our spies have reported your involvement in secret meetings with known dissenters. How do you respond to these accusations?"

Erik's face remained inscrutable, though a flicker of surprise crossed his eyes. "I have been loyal to you, my king. These accusations are false. I have only acted in the interest of the kingdom and its stability."

Eirik's gaze did not waver. "The evidence suggests otherwise. If you are innocent, you will have no problem proving it. But if you are guilty, know that the penalty for betrayal is severe."

Thord, standing beside Jarl Erik, looked equally composed. "My king," he said, his voice firm, "I have served you faithfully. These accusations are baseless. I swear upon my honor that I am loyal to you."

Eirik studied them both, his mind weighing their words and the evidence he had seen. The stakes were high, and he knew that any misstep could have dire consequences. The integrity of his rule depended on his ability to identify and deal with treachery swiftly.

"I will give you an opportunity to clear your names," Eirik said finally. "You will both be placed under close watch, and any further evidence of disloyalty will be met with the harshest punishment."

With that, Jarl Erik and Thord were dismissed, their faces a mixture of relief and lingering suspicion. Eirik watched them leave, his mind already turning to the next steps in dealing with the threat of betrayal.

In the days that followed, Skarde and his team conducted a covert investigation into the conspiracy. They uncovered more evidence of secret meetings and clandestine communications, painting a clearer picture of the extent of the betrayal. It became evident that Jarl Erik and Thord were indeed involved in a plot to undermine Eirik's rule, although the full scope of their plans remained unclear.

Eirik's patience wore thin as he waited for the final pieces of the puzzle to fall into place. He knew that the time for action was approaching, and he was prepared to act decisively. The consequences for those who betrayed him would be severe, a warning to others who might consider challenging his authority.

The night before the planned confrontation, Eirik sat alone in his chambers, his thoughts a whirlwind of strategy and resolve. He knew that the execution of his plans would require both precision and ruthlessness. The betrayal he faced was a test of his strength and cunning, and he was determined to pass it with unwavering resolve.

As he prepared for the confrontation, Eirik's thoughts turned to the broader implications of the betrayal. The web of intrigue and ambition that surrounded him was complex and treacherous, but he was ready to navigate it with the same cold determination that had brought him to the throne. The kingdom of Norway was his to shape, and he would use every tool at his disposal to secure his rule and eliminate any threats to his power.

The following morning, Eirik called another council meeting, this time with a sense of grim finality. The great hall was filled with the key figures of his court, their faces a mix of curiosity and apprehension. Eirik knew that this meeting would be a turning point, and he intended to make an example of those who had betrayed him.

As the council assembled, Eirik took his place at the head of the table, his expression a mask of cold determination. The fate of Jarl Erik and Thord would be decided here, and Eirik was prepared to demonstrate the full extent of his authority.

Chapter 12
Turmoil of Rule

The frost of winter had not yet fully gripped Norway, but the kingdom was already steeped in a chilling atmosphere of unrest and bloodshed. Eirik Bloodaxe's reign, which had begun with the promise of unity, was increasingly marked by a relentless spiral into violence and chaos. His efforts to consolidate power were met with fierce resistance, and the brutal measures he employed only served to deepen the fractures within his realm.

The city of Nidaros, once a symbol of Eirik's newfound dominance, had become a stage for increasingly brutal displays of power. The great hall, now a grim chamber of judgment, was filled with whispers of fear and conspiracy. Eirik's attempts to impose his rule had resulted in a series of harsh and bloody actions designed to quash any sign of dissent.

Rumors of an uprising had reached Eirik's ears. The southern regions, which had long been a bedrock of resistance, were now seething with unrest. The chieftains in these areas, many of whom had been marginalized or outright antagonized by Eirik's brutal consolidation of power, were increasingly vocal in their opposition. Their growing defiance was a clear threat to Eirik's authority.

The king's response was swift and merciless. He ordered a series of punitive expeditions to the south, led by his most trusted commanders. These expeditions were designed not just to suppress rebellion but to send a clear message of Eirik's uncompromising stance. The result was a wave of violence that left the southern regions scarred and subdued.

One such expedition was led by Jarl Torstein, a formidable warrior loyal to Eirik. Torstein's forces descended upon a village in the southern part of Norway that was rumored to be a hotbed of dissent. The village, nestled in a picturesque valley, was soon engulfed in a scene of terror.

Under Torstein's command, the village was surrounded and its inhabitants were given a grim ultimatum: pledge allegiance to Eirik or face the consequences. The villagers, many of whom were simple farmers and traders, had little choice but to comply. But the show of force was not merely a matter of enforcement; it was a demonstration of the king's willingness to use extreme measures to maintain control.

When the villagers hesitated, the consequences were swift and brutal. Torstein's men, with their swords and axes gleaming in the cold light, stormed through the village. Buildings were set ablaze, livestock was slaughtered, and the air was filled with the screams of the innocent. The brutality of the attack left no doubt about the consequences of defiance. The village was reduced to ashes, and its survivors were left to grapple with the aftermath of Eirik's ruthless enforcement.

The violence extended beyond the battlefield. Eirik's court was rife with intrigue and suspicion. Those who were perceived to be potential threats were dealt with harshly. One evening, Eirik summoned several prominent chieftains to the great hall under the guise of a council meeting. The atmosphere was tense, and the chieftains, though outwardly respectful, were on edge.

As the meeting progressed, Eirik's demeanor grew increasingly menacing. His eyes, cold and calculating, surveyed the room with a sense of predatory vigilance. Without warning, Eirik accused several of the chieftains of conspiring against him. The evidence he presented was circumstantial, but the decision was already made. The accused were seized by Eirik's guards and taken away, their fate sealed by the king's ruthless judgment.

The subsequent days saw a series of public executions. Eirik made an example of those he deemed traitors, parading them through the streets before executing them in a manner designed to instill fear. The brutality of the executions was a stark reminder of the price of opposition. Heads were displayed on pikes, and the gruesome spectacle was a grim testament to Eirik's determination to suppress any challenge to his rule.

Amidst this violence, the relationship between Eirik and his brother Haakon had deteriorated further. Haakon's disillusionment with Eirik's reign had reached a breaking point. The increasing bloodshed and the harsh measures employed by Eirik had driven Haakon to seek refuge elsewhere. His decision to leave Norway was not just a personal escape but also a political maneuver.

Haakon's departure was a significant blow to Eirik's reign. Once a symbol of unity within the royal family, Haakon's exit was seen as a clear sign of Eirik's faltering control. The southern chieftains, emboldened by Haakon's defection, saw an opportunity to further challenge Eirik's authority.

As Haakon made his way to England, the journey itself was fraught with danger. The political landscape of England was complex, and Haakon had to navigate a web of alliances and rivalries to secure his place. His arrival was met with a mixture of curiosity and skepticism. The English court, aware of the turmoil in Norway, saw Haakon's presence as both a potential asset and a threat.

In England, Haakon sought support from influential figures who might help him regain his position or provide him with a new role. His attempts to build alliances were met with varying degrees of success. Some saw him as a potential ally, while others viewed him with suspicion. Haakon's presence in England added a new layer of complexity to the already volatile political situation.

Back in Norway, the violence continued unabated. Eirik's reign was increasingly characterized by a cycle of brutality and repression. The kingdom was a land divided, with the southern regions simmering with resistance and the northern areas under a constant state of fear. The harsh measures taken by Eirik had created a climate of instability that threatened to unravel the fragile peace he had imposed.

The kingdom's suffering was a testament to the high cost of Eirik's rule. The violence that had marked his reign was not merely a series of isolated incidents but a pervasive feature of his governance. The brutality of his methods had alienated many of his former allies and fueled the growing opposition.

As winter continued to tighten its grip on Norway, Eirik faced the daunting challenge of addressing the unrest and restoring stability. The kingdom was in turmoil.

Chapter 13
Fires of Rebellion

Spring had arrived, bringing with it a reluctant thaw that struggled to dispel the chill that gripped Norway—not just from the lingering winter but from the deep-seated unrest within the kingdom. Eirik Bloodaxe's reign, marked by a relentless cycle of violence and repression, had only grown more tumultuous as the days lengthened. His harsh rule had not quelled the dissent but had instead fanned the flames of rebellion, particularly in the southern regions, where discontent had coalesced into organized resistance.

The kingdom's landscape was dotted with the scars of Eirik's brutal consolidation of power. Villages burned, fields lay fallow, and the people lived in a state of perpetual fear. The southern chieftains, once subdued, were now rallying under a common cause: the overthrow of Eirik's tyrannical rule. Their growing unity posed a serious threat to the king's authority.

In the heart of the southern resistance was a charismatic chieftain named Rolf, a man known for his strategic acumen and fierce independence. Rolf had managed to unite several of the disaffected chieftains and common folk into a formidable force. His leadership had transformed scattered opposition into a cohesive army, determined to challenge Eirik's dominance.

Rolf's insurgent force had begun to mount increasingly bold attacks against Eirik's garrisons and supply lines. Small skirmishes had turned into larger battles, and the southern resistance began to threaten the stability of Eirik's hold on the region. The king's response was swift and ruthless, deploying his most seasoned commanders to quell the uprising.

One such commander was Jarl Torstein, who had previously demonstrated his effectiveness in suppressing dissent. Torstein was now tasked with crushing the southern rebellion once and for all. His forces, well-equipped and battle-hardened, marched south with a grim determination to restore order by any means necessary.

The conflict came to a head at a place called Skjoldheim, a strategic village that lay at the crossroads of several key supply routes. The village had become a stronghold for Rolf and his followers, and its capture was crucial to Eirik's efforts to quell the rebellion. Torstein's approach was swift and brutal, aiming to strike fear into the hearts of the resistance and dismantle their base of operations.

As Torstein's army encircled Skjoldheim, the village braced itself for the impending assault. The defenders, though outnumbered, were resolute. Rolf had fortified the village with makeshift defenses and prepared his men for the inevitable clash. The battle that ensued was fierce and bloody, with the air filled with the sounds of clashing steel and the cries of the wounded.

Torstein's tactics were ruthless. He ordered his men to lay siege to the village, cutting off all supply lines and bombarding the defenses with siege engines. The villagers, who had already endured months of hardship, were now facing the full force of Eirik's wrath. The siege lasted for several days, with both sides suffering heavy casualties.

The final assault came with a ferocity that left no room for mercy. Torstein's forces launched a coordinated attack, breaching the village's defenses and pouring into Skjoldheim. The battle turned into a massacre, with the streets running red with blood. Rolf and his most loyal warriors fought desperately to defend their stronghold, but the overwhelming numbers and the sheer brutality of the assault took their toll.

In the chaos, Rolf was captured. His defiance and leadership had made him a prime target, and

Torstein took no pleasure in the capture but saw it as a necessary step in asserting Eirik's dominance. The chieftain was bound and brought before Torstein, his face smeared with blood and dirt, but his eyes still burning with defiance.

Torstein, standing amidst the carnage, regarded Rolf with a steely gaze. "Your resistance ends here," he declared. "Eirik Bloodaxe has no tolerance for rebellion, and you will pay the price for your defiance."

Rolf's response was defiant. "Eirik is a tyrant," he spat. "His rule is built on fear and bloodshed. The people will rise against him, even if I am not there to lead them."

Torstein's expression remained impassive. "Your words will not save you. The fate of those who defy Eirik is well known."

Rolf's capture marked a turning point in the rebellion. The fall of Skjoldheim and the capture of its leader sent a clear message to the other chieftains and resistance fighters. Eirik's regime was unyielding and would not tolerate any challenge to its authority. The king's grip on the southern regions was strengthened, but the cost of victory was high. The brutality of the siege had left a trail of devastation, further alienating the people and fueling the cycle of resentment and violence.

In the aftermath of the battle, Eirik's forces conducted a series of reprisals against the villages and towns that had supported the rebellion. The king's desire to make an example of those who had resisted him led to further acts of cruelty. The public executions of captured rebels and suspected sympathizers were meant to demonstrate the consequences of defying Eirik's rule. The once-proud resistance had been crushed, but the scars of the conflict would linger long after the last of the fires had died out.

The brutality of Eirik's methods continued to create a volatile environment within the kingdom. While he had managed to suppress the immediate threat of rebellion, the underlying discontent and resistance remained. The cycle of violence that marked his reign was far from over, and the kingdom of Norway was left grappling with the consequences of Eirik Bloodaxe's ruthless rule.

As the spring thaw continued, the harsh reality of Eirik's reign became increasingly apparent. The kingdom was a land scarred by conflict and repression, and the king's attempts to maintain control were met with a growing sense of disillusionment and resistance. Eirik's reign was defined by a relentless pursuit of power and a willingness to use violence to achieve his goals. The fires of rebellion had been quelled for now, but the shadow of discontent continued to loom over Norway.

Chapter 14
Cracks in the Iron Crown

The summer sun barely warmed the cold landscape of Norway, where the aftermath of Eirik Bloodaxe's brutal campaign had left deep scars. The defeat of Rolf and the southern rebellion had only temporarily quelled the unrest. Despite Eirik's show of force, the kingdom was rife with underlying tension. His iron-fisted rule, marked by bloodshed and intimidation, had not won him the loyalty he craved. Instead, it had fostered resentment and unrest that threatened to undermine his reign.

In the wake of the southern campaign, Eirik turned his attention to consolidating his gains and addressing the growing discontent within his court and among the people. His once-strong alliances were starting to fray, and the stability of his rule was increasingly in question. The brutal repression had alienated many of his former supporters, and whispers of dissent grew louder by the day.

The king's court, once a place of strategic discussion and alliances, had become a theater of intrigue and distrust. Eirik's need to maintain control led him to suspect everyone around him, and paranoia seeped into his decisions. The nobility, who had initially supported him out of fear or personal gain, now faced the brunt of Eirik's suspicions and demands.

One evening, as the sun dipped below the horizon, casting long shadows over the great hall of Nidaros, Eirik convened a council meeting with his closest advisors and loyal chieftains. The room was heavy with the scent of roasted meats and the murmurs of anxious courtiers. Eirik's gaze swept over the assembled nobles, his expression stern and unyielding.

"Recent events have shown that our enemies are not just outside our walls but within them," Eirik declared, his voice echoing through the hall. "I cannot afford to be complacent. We must root out every trace of disloyalty and ensure that our control remains unchallenged."

The council members shifted uneasily in their seats. Eirik's reputation for ruthlessness had created an atmosphere of fear, and any hint of dissent could be fatal. The king's recent campaigns had been brutal, but his actions within the court were equally unforgiving.

Eirik's focus was particularly intense on the chieftains who had once been loyal but were now seen as potential threats. Among them was Jarl Sigurd, a once-prominent supporter who had fallen out of favor. Sigurd's lands were rumored to be a hotbed of discontent, and Eirik was determined to address the perceived threat with decisive action.

"Jarl Sigurd," Eirik said, his eyes narrowing as he addressed the jarl directly, "you have been a trusted ally, but I have received troubling reports about your loyalty. I need to know where you stand. Are you with me, or do you harbor ambitions of your own?"

Sigurd's face remained impassive, but his hands clenched into fists. "My loyalty to the crown is unquestionable," he replied, his voice steady. "I have served you faithfully, and my lands are a testament to that."

Eirik's expression did not soften. "Loyalty must be proven, not merely professed. I cannot afford to take chances. If there is any doubt, it must be removed."

The tension in the room was palpable. Eirik's willingness to question even his most trusted allies was a clear indication of the level of paranoia that now characterized his rule. Sigurd, feeling the weight of Eirik's scrutiny, knew that his position was precarious.

The following day, Eirik's men were dispatched to Jarl Sigurd's lands under the guise of a routine inspection. The true purpose of the visit, however, was to gather evidence of any possible disloyalty and to intimidate Sigurd's supporters. The inspection turned into a thorough search, with Eirik's guards interrogating Sigurd's retainers and scrutinizing every corner of his estate.

The search yielded little concrete evidence of disloyalty, but the show of force was meant to send a clear message. Sigurd's lands were subjected to a series of punitive measures, including the seizure of resources and the imposition of heavy fines. The jarl's wealth and influence were significantly diminished, a stark reminder of the consequences of crossing Eirik Bloodaxe.

The punitive measures against Sigurd were only the beginning. Eirik's reign continued to be marked by a series of increasingly harsh actions aimed at consolidating his control. The kingdom's nobles and chieftains faced mounting pressure to demonstrate their loyalty, and any hint of dissent was met with swift and brutal reprisals.

The public's discontent was also growing. The harsh measures and the brutal campaigns had left the common people weary and fearful. The streets of Nidaros, once bustling with activity, were now quieter as the people avoided attracting the king's attention. Rumors of famine and hardship were becoming more common, further fueling dissatisfaction.

In this climate of fear and repression, Eirik sought to bolster his position through a series of strategic marriages and alliances. His attempt to secure his rule through these alliances was driven by a need to offset the growing opposition. Marriages to influential families were meant to strengthen his position, but they also highlighted the king's increasing desperation to secure his power.

Despite Eirik's efforts, the cracks in his rule were becoming more apparent. The kingdom was deeply divided, with regions and factions increasingly at odds with one another. Eirik's reliance on fear and brutality had not secured the loyalty he needed; instead, it had deepened the divisions within his realm.

One particularly grim night, the king's paranoia reached a new level. Eirik summoned his most trusted advisors to a clandestine meeting. The setting was a dimly lit chamber beneath the great hall, far from the prying eyes of the court. The walls of the chamber were adorned with crude tapestries, and the air was thick with the scent of burning oil.

Eirik, seated at the head of the table, leaned forward, his face illuminated by the flickering light. "We face threats on all sides," he said, his voice low and intense. "I need to know that we are united in our efforts to maintain control. Any sign of weakness could be our downfall."

The advisors exchanged uneasy glances, their loyalty tested by Eirik's demands. The king's increasing paranoia was a source of concern, and the atmosphere in the chamber was tense. Eirik's quest for absolute control had left him isolated, even among those who were meant to be his closest allies.

The meeting concluded with Eirik reaffirming his determination to root out any threats to his rule.

Chapter 15
Whispering Shadows

Autumn had deepened, casting long shadows over the cold, rugged landscape of Norway. The kingdom, still reeling from the aftermath of Eirik Bloodaxe's brutal campaign against the southern rebels, now faced new challenges. The harsh winter loomed on the horizon, promising to compound the suffering of the people. Eirik's rule, marked by cruelty and suspicion, had driven the kingdom into a state of uneasy calm, but the cracks in his reign continued to widen.

In the remote highlands of Norway, a different kind of unrest was brewing. The rugged terrain and dense forests had become a refuge for those who opposed Eirik's rule. Outlaws, disaffected chieftains, and former rebels had banded together in a loose confederation, their grievances fueling their resistance against the king's harsh regime. Among them was a man known only as Grim, a leader whose reputation for cunning and ruthlessness was rivaled only by Eirik himself.

Grim's band of outlaws had become a thorn in Eirik's side, launching hit-and-run attacks on supply caravans and small garrisons scattered across the highlands. Their actions were not only a direct challenge to Eirik's authority but also a symbol of the growing unrest among those who had suffered under his rule. The outlaws operated with a level of coordination and effectiveness that caught the king's attention.

In response to these mounting threats, Eirik assembled a force to address the growing problem in the highlands. He tasked his most trusted commander, Jarl Torstein, with the mission of eradicating the outlaw threat. Torstein, whose brutal tactics had previously quelled the southern rebellion, was now expected to apply the same level of ferocity to the highland insurgents.

As Torstein and his troops prepared for the campaign, the atmosphere within the king's court was tense. Eirik's advisors and courtiers watched with a mixture of apprehension and anticipation. The king's focus on quelling the highland threat was seen as a necessary step to consolidate his rule, but the growing unrest among the populace raised concerns about the sustainability of his approach.

The highland campaign began with a series of coordinated raids. Torstein's forces, equipped with siege weapons and supplies, moved swiftly through the rugged terrain. Their goal was not only to defeat Grim's band but to strike terror into any potential supporters of the outlaw leader. The king's strategy was clear: eliminate the insurgents and make an example of those who defied his rule.

Grim, aware of Torstein's approach, had taken measures to prepare for the inevitable clash. His band had fortified their hideouts and set traps throughout the highlands. The outlaws used the harsh terrain to their advantage, launching guerrilla attacks and using their knowledge of the land to evade the king's forces. The highland campaign became a grueling battle of attrition, with both sides suffering heavy losses.

One particularly brutal clash occurred in a narrow mountain pass known as the Wyrm's Teeth, a strategic location that Grim had chosen for its natural defenses. Torstein's forces, determined to flush out the outlaws, engaged in a fierce battle with Grim's men. The narrow pass turned into a chaotic battlefield, with the sounds of clashing steel and the screams of the wounded echoing through the mountains.

Torstein's troops advanced with grim determination, their heavy armor and shields providing some protection against the outlaws' arrows and hit-and-run tactics. The battle raged on for hours, with both sides locked in a desperate struggle. Despite their numerical advantage, Torstein's forces faced significant challenges due to the difficult terrain and the tenacity of Grim's band.

As the battle reached its climax, Grim himself appeared on the battlefield, leading a counterattack against the king's forces. His presence was a rallying point for the outlaws, and his ferocious combat skills turned the tide of the battle in their favor. Torstein, recognizing the significance of Grim's leadership, ordered a concentrated assault to eliminate the outlaw leader.

The clash between Torstein and Grim was a dramatic confrontation, each man embodying the fierce determination and brutality that had marked their respective campaigns. The two warriors faced off amidst the chaos of battle, their swords clashing with a force that reverberated through the air. The duel was intense and brutal, with neither side willing to give an inch.

In the midst of the chaos, Torstein's forces managed to gain the upper hand, slowly pushing Grim's band back. The battle was a bloody and costly affair, with both sides suffering heavy casualties. Grim's outlaws, despite their resilience, were eventually forced to retreat, leaving behind a field littered with the dead and wounded.

The aftermath of the battle left the highlands in a state of devastation. Torstein's forces, victorious but weary, began the grim task of mopping up the remnants of Grim's band. The king's campaign had succeeded in its immediate objective, but the cost of victory was high. The highland region was left scarred and traumatized, with the people suffering from the aftermath of the brutal conflict.

Eirik's response to the campaign was both triumphant and ominous. The king saw the highland campaign as a necessary step in consolidating his rule, but the growing opposition and unrest continued to pose a threat. The kingdom remained a land of deep divisions, with the brutality of Eirik's reign fueling ongoing resistance and resentment.

As the autumn leaves fell, the situation in Norway remained fraught with tension. Eirik's rule was marked by a cycle of violence and repression, with each campaign and clash adding to the instability of the kingdom. The highlands, once a symbol of resistance, had been subdued, but the underlying discontent and opposition persisted.

The fires of rebellion burned brightly in the hearts of those who had suffered under Eirik's rule.

Chapter 16
Fall of the Crown

Winter had settled over Norway like a heavy shroud, its icy grip tightening on the land and its people. The snow-covered landscape was a stark contrast to the tumultuous events that had unfolded in recent months. Eirik Bloodaxe's rule, once marked by a display of relentless force and brutality, was now facing an unforeseen and dire turn of events.

The king's reign, strained by constant unrest and rebellion, had begun to unravel. The highland campaign had been a costly endeavor, and while it had subdued the immediate threat, it had not resolved the underlying issues. The relentless pressure from internal dissent and the burden of ongoing conflicts had taken a toll on Eirik's rule. The kingdom was increasingly unstable, and the king's grip on power was weakening.

In the midst of this turmoil, Eirik's brothers, who had once been his rivals, saw an opportunity to act. Haakon, who had taken refuge in England, had been a thorn in Eirik's side since his departure. The exiled brother had managed to secure support from the English court, where he had formed alliances and gathered resources. Haakon's presence in England was a constant reminder of the fractured state of the royal family and the lingering threat to Eirik's rule.

The English court, under the influence of Haakon and other disaffected factions, saw the opportunity to undermine Eirik's authority. The English king, Edward the Elder, was aware of the unrest in Norway and saw the situation as a chance to weaken a potential adversary. With the backing of Haakon and the support of key English nobles, a plan was set in motion to remove Eirik from the throne.

News of the growing opposition reached Eirik's court, where his advisors and nobles were increasingly wary of the king's position. The internal divisions and the persistent threat from abroad had created a precarious situation. The king's once-mighty power seemed to be slipping through his fingers.

As winter deepened, the English launched a series of strategic attacks along the Norwegian coastline. Their goal was to destabilize Eirik's control and to support the claims of Haakon and other opposition leaders. The English forces, well-equipped and organized, began to seize key coastal towns and disrupt Eirik's supply lines.

Eirik, caught off guard by the sudden escalation, struggled to respond effectively. His forces, already stretched thin by the recent campaigns and internal strife, were ill-prepared for a full-scale invasion. The king's attempts to rally his troops and mount a defense were met with increasing resistance from both external enemies and internal dissenters.

The situation reached a critical point when English forces, led by a seasoned commander named Ealdred, landed in the town of Nidaros. The town, once a symbol of Eirik's power, had become a focal point of the conflict. Ealdred's forces quickly overran the town, facing only token resistance from Eirik's beleaguered garrison.

With Nidaros falling into enemy hands, the pressure on Eirik intensified. The king's advisors and nobles, recognizing the inevitability of defeat, began to consider their own positions. The prospect of a new ruler and the shifting balance of power created an atmosphere of uncertainty and trepidation within the court.

In a desperate move, Eirik decided to take drastic action. He summoned his most trusted supporters and began preparations for a retreat. The king's plan was to flee to the northern territories, where he hoped to regroup and find allies willing to support his cause. His departure was shrouded in secrecy, with only a few loyalists aware of the full extent of his plans.

As Eirik and his retinue made their way north, the journey was fraught with peril. The harsh winter weather and the constant threat of pursuit from English forces and rival factions made the escape a desperate and dangerous endeavor. The king's progress was slow, and the harsh conditions took a toll on both men and horses.

Eirik's flight was marked by a series of narrow escapes and confrontations. The king's attempts to find sanctuary in the northern territories were met with mixed success. Some local chieftains were sympathetic to Eirik's plight, but others were eager to distance themselves from the fallen king and align themselves with the emerging powers.

Eventually, Eirik's efforts to secure a foothold in Norway proved fruitless. The combined forces of the English and Haakon's supporters had effectively cut off his avenues of escape. Facing the reality of his predicament, Eirik was left with no choice but to seek refuge beyond the shores of Norway.

The king's final destination was the British Isles, where Haakon had established a presence. The decision to seek refuge in England was both a strategic and personal one. Eirik hoped to find sanctuary among those who had once been his rivals, hoping for a chance to negotiate his future and perhaps reclaim his position.

Upon arriving in England, Eirik was met with a mixture of apprehension and cautious welcome. Haakon, now a key figure in the English court, was instrumental in securing Eirik's position. The former king of Norway found himself in an unfamiliar and precarious situation, reliant on the support of those who had once been his enemies.

Haakon, though wary of his brother, understood the value of maintaining an alliance. The two men, now united by their shared plight, engaged in negotiations with the English court. Eirik's presence in England created a diplomatic dilemma, and the court had to weigh the implications of harboring a former king and rival.

The winter continued to exert its harsh influence, both on the land and on Eirik's fortunes. The former king of Norway, once a figure of immense power and fear, was now a displaced and disillusioned figure. The harsh reality of his fall from power had set in, and the consequences of his brutal reign were becoming increasingly apparent.

In the shadow of the English court, Eirik's future remained uncertain. The political landscape of the British Isles was shifting, and the former king had to navigate the complexities of his new environment.

The remnants of Eirik's once-mighty rule were now a distant memory, overshadowed by the new challenges and alliances that lay ahead.

As the first snows of winter blanketed the British Isles, Eirik Bloodaxe faced the stark reality of his exile. The king who had once commanded fear and respect was now a figure of historical interest and political intrigue. The fires of rebellion that had marked his reign had not only shaped the course of Norwegian history but had also left an indelible mark on his own fate.

Chapter 17
A Warlord's Ascendancy

Spring had finally arrived, and with it, a new chapter in Eirik Bloodaxe's turbulent life. The icy grip of winter had begun to thaw, revealing the lush, green landscape of the British Isles. For Eirik, the shift in seasons marked not only a change in weather but also the beginning of a renewed quest for power. The exiled king, now a warlord in a foreign land, sought to reforge his destiny and reclaim his former glory through new alliances and relentless raiding.

Eirik's arrival in the British Isles had been met with a mixture of suspicion and curiosity. The English court had initially viewed him as a figure of potential trouble, a displaced Viking king who might bring more chaos to their shores. However, Eirik's reputation and experience as a formidable warrior were undeniable, and he quickly made his presence felt among the local factions.

In the early months of his exile, Eirik established himself among the Viking communities that had settled in the northern territories of the British Isles. These communities, still steeped in the old ways of raiding and conquest, welcomed Eirik as a leader who could guide them to new opportunities. The Viking settlements in Northumbria and beyond had long been known for their fierce independence and martial prowess, making them fertile ground for Eirik's ambitions.

With a growing band of loyal followers and a renewed sense of purpose, Eirik set about organizing a series of raids along the coastlines of the British Isles. His strategy was to build his reputation as a warlord and to demonstrate his continued relevance in the realm of Viking conquest. Eirik's raids were swift and brutal, targeting coastal towns and monasteries known for their wealth and strategic value.

The raids were meticulously planned and executed with the precision that had once defined Eirik's campaigns in Norway. His forces, equipped with longships and the latest weaponry, struck with a ferocity that left their targets in disarray. The Viking raiders were relentless, their attacks marked by the same ruthless efficiency that had characterized Eirik's rule back in Norway.

One notable raid took place on the coastal town of Whitby, a strategic location known for its wealth and religious significance. Eirik's forces descended upon the town with a speed that caught the defenders off guard. The raid was a brutal display of Viking power, with Eirik's men seizing valuable goods and capturing prisoners. The swift and decisive nature of the raid earned Eirik both fear and respect among the local population.

The success of Eirik's raids did not go unnoticed by the political landscape of the British Isles. The King of Northumbria, a shrewd and calculating ruler named Æthelstan, recognized the potential benefits of aligning with Eirik. Northumbria, a kingdom marked by its own struggles with external threats and internal divisions, saw in Eirik a valuable ally who could help consolidate power and counterbalance rival factions.

Æthelstan, eager to strengthen his position and secure his kingdom against the encroaching forces of the English and other Viking groups, sought to form an alliance with Eirik. The two leaders met in a covert gathering, away from the prying eyes of their respective courts. The meeting took place in a secluded forest clearing, where the rustling leaves and the distant call of birds created an atmosphere of quiet determination.

Eirik, clad in his battle-worn armor and accompanied by his trusted advisors, faced Æthelstan with a mixture of skepticism and resolve. The King of Northumbria, dressed in fine, richly embroidered robes, greeted Eirik with a measured nod.

"Eirik Bloodaxe," Æthelstan began, his voice calm and authoritative, "your reputation precedes you. The raids you have conducted have shown that you remain a force to be reckoned with. Northumbria finds itself in a precarious position, and I believe that an alliance between us could be mutually beneficial."

Eirik regarded Æthelstan with a scrutinizing gaze. The king's words were carefully chosen, reflecting both the potential advantages and the underlying political maneuvering. "I have heard of Northumbria's struggles and the strength you command," Eirik replied. "An alliance could serve us both well, but we must be clear on the terms."

Æthelstan nodded in agreement. "Our interests align in several ways. By joining forces, we can secure our respective territories and challenge those who seek to undermine us. Your raiding experience and military prowess are assets I value. In return, I offer support for your continued endeavors and a position of influence within my court."

The terms of the alliance were discussed and agreed upon. Eirik's role in Northumbria was defined as a prominent warlord and military leader. He was given command over a contingent of Northumbrian forces and granted a degree of autonomy in his raiding activities. The alliance also included mutual support in military campaigns and the sharing of resources.

The formal alliance was solidified with a ceremony that marked the beginning of a new chapter for Eirik. The ceremony took place in a grand hall in Northumbria, where Eirik and Æthelstan were publicly recognized as allies. The event was attended by key figures from both sides, and the atmosphere was one of cautious optimism.

With the alliance secured, Eirik wasted no time in leveraging his new position. He continued his raiding activities with renewed vigor, now bolstered by the resources and support of Northumbria. The raids targeted key locations along the northern coasts of England, striking at rival factions and securing valuable spoils.

Eirik's activities as a warlord began to shift the balance of power in the British Isles. His raids disrupted the stability of neighboring regions and contributed to the growing influence of Northumbria. The king's alliance with Eirik was paying dividends, with the former king of Norway proving to be a formidable asset in the struggle for dominance.

Despite his new role and the apparent success of his endeavors, Eirik remained acutely aware of the precarious nature of his situation. The political landscape of the British Isles was dynamic and unpredictable, and the alliances he forged were subject to change. Eirik's position as a warlord was a double-edged sword, offering both opportunities and risks.

As summer approached, Eirik's reputation continued to grow. His raids had become legendary, and his influence in Northumbria was solidified. However, the complexities of his new environment and the ever-present threat of shifting allegiances meant that Eirik could never fully relax. The former king of Norway had found a new battleground, and his quest for power was far from over.

In the shadow of Northumbria's rising power, Eirik Bloodaxe navigated the treacherous waters of his new role.

Chapter 18
The Fall of a Warlord

The summer of 948 brought with it a profound sense of unease across the British Isles. Eirik Bloodaxe, having firmly established himself as a formidable warlord, had quickly become a significant player in the political landscape of Northumbria. His alliance with King Æthelstan had bolstered Northumbria's strength, and his relentless raiding had garnered both fear and respect. However, the shifting tides of power in the British Isles were about to bring a dramatic turn of events.

The dominant force behind this new shift was King Eadred of the Anglo-Saxon kingdom of England. Eadred, who had recently ascended to the throne, was determined to assert control over the northern territories, including Northumbria. His ambition was clear: to consolidate English control over the north and to eliminate any threats that stood in the way of a unified English realm.

Eadred's approach was methodical and strategic. He recognized the growing influence of Eirik Bloodaxe and saw the Viking warlord as a significant obstacle to his plans. The new king was determined to remove Eirik from Northumbria and reassert English dominance in the region. To this end, Eadred initiated a series of moves designed to undermine Eirik's position and prepare for a decisive confrontation.

The first step in Eadred's strategy was to rally support among the Anglo-Saxon nobles and regional leaders who were discontent with Eirik's presence. Many of these leaders viewed Eirik as an interloper and were eager to see him removed. Eadred's diplomacy was skillful; he promised rewards and incentives to those who supported his efforts to expel the Viking warlord. The king's efforts bore fruit, and a coalition of disaffected nobles began to form in opposition to Eirik's rule.

In addition to political maneuvering, Eadred employed military tactics to weaken Eirik's position. The king's forces, led by seasoned commanders, began to conduct targeted raids against Viking-held territories. These raids aimed to disrupt Eirik's supply lines, reduce his resources, and demoralize his followers. The Anglo-Saxon strategy was to create a situation where Eirik would be forced to fight on multiple fronts, stretching his forces thin and diminishing his ability to maintain control.

Eirik, ever vigilant, was aware of the growing threat from the south. His advisors and scouts reported increasing activity among Eadred's forces, and the signs of a coordinated effort to undermine his position became apparent. Despite his formidable military reputation, Eirik faced a challenging situation. The political and military landscape was shifting against him, and the support he had relied on was increasingly in jeopardy.

One pivotal confrontation occurred in the early autumn, when Eadred's forces launched a major offensive against a key Viking stronghold in the region. The town of York, a strategic location under Eirik's control, became the focal point of the conflict. The siege of York was a decisive battle that would determine the outcome of Eirik's position in Northumbria.

The siege was conducted with precision and brutality. Eadred's forces, equipped with siege weapons and supported by a formidable contingent of archers and infantry, surrounded York and cut off its supply routes. The town's defenders, led by Eirik's most trusted commanders, faced a grueling and desperate struggle. The once-vibrant town was now a scene of chaos and conflict, with the sounds of battle echoing through the streets.

Eirik, determined to hold his ground, took command of the defense. The battle was fierce, with both sides engaging in a brutal exchange of attacks and counterattacks. The defenders, though fiercely loyal, were outnumbered and increasingly exhausted. Eirik's leadership and combat skills were on full display, but the pressure from Eadred's forces was unrelenting.

As the siege continued, the situation for Eirik became increasingly dire. The town's defenses began to crumble under the relentless assault, and the morale of the defenders waned. The Viking warlord, realizing the gravity of the situation, attempted to negotiate with Eadred's forces, seeking terms that might allow for a dignified retreat. However, Eadred was resolute in his determination to expel Eirik from Northumbria and refused to offer favorable terms.

The final assault on York came with a ferocity that left little room for mercy. Eadred's forces breached the town's defenses and poured into the streets, engaging in brutal hand-to-hand combat with the remaining defenders. The town, once a symbol of Eirik's power, was reduced to a battlefield of blood and fire.

Eirik, facing the collapse of his position, made a strategic retreat. The Viking warlord withdrew from York with what remained of his forces, leaving behind a city ravaged by the conflict. The retreat was a desperate maneuver, intended to preserve his remaining strength and seek refuge elsewhere.

The fall of York marked a significant turning point in Eirik's campaign. The loss of the town and the defeat of his forces dealt a severe blow to Eirik's ambitions in Northumbria. Eadred's victory was a decisive factor in the consolidation of Anglo-Saxon control over the northern territories. The king's determination to remove Eirik from the British Isles had succeeded, and the Viking warlord was left to face the consequences of his ousting.

Eirik's options were now severely limited. The political and military landscape of the British Isles had shifted dramatically, and the former king of Norway faced the reality of his exile. The once-feared warlord, who had sought to carve out a new realm for himself, was now a displaced and hunted figure.

In the wake of his defeat, Eirik attempted to regroup and seek new opportunities. He traveled through the northern regions, seeking refuge among Viking communities and exploring potential alliances. However, the political climate was hostile, and the options for a resurgence were limited. The Viking warlord, once a commanding figure in the British Isles, now faced the harsh reality of his diminished status.

As the winter of 949 approached, Eirik Bloodaxe found himself on the fringes of a realm that had once been his battleground. The ambitions and dreams of conquest that had driven him were now tempered by the harsh reality of defeat. The political and military landscape of the British Isles had shifted, and the warlord who had once sought to dominate was now a figure of historical interest and political intrigue.

Chapter 19
A Brief Resurgence

The new year of 950 brought with it an unexpected twist in the turbulent saga of Eirik Bloodaxe. Despite his recent defeat and exile from Northumbria, the Viking warlord was far from finished. His reputation, though tarnished, still carried weight among those who sought to challenge the existing power structures. The political landscape in the British Isles remained fluid, and Eirik saw an opportunity to reclaim what he had lost.

Eirik's return to the British Isles was marked by a calculated resurgence. The Viking warlord, having spent several months regrouping and strategizing, had managed to gather a small but determined force of loyal followers. His aim was clear: to return to Northumbria and reassert his control over the region. The political instability and shifting alliances in the British Isles provided the perfect backdrop for his comeback.

The initial phase of Eirik's campaign involved a series of strategic maneuvers aimed at destabilizing the English-held territories. He targeted key towns and fortresses along the northern coast, conducting surprise raids and skirmishes that disrupted the English administration and undermined their control. Eirik's tactics were ruthless and effective, designed to create chaos and sow dissent among the English and their allies.

One notable action was a raid on the town of Newcastle. Eirik's forces, using their knowledge of the local terrain and employing their trademark ferocity, quickly overran the town's defenses. The raid was brutal and swift, with Eirik's men seizing valuable resources and taking prisoners. The success of the raid sent a clear message: Eirik Bloodaxe was back and ready to reclaim his position.

The impact of Eirik's resurgence was felt across Northumbria. The English authorities, caught off guard by the sudden and aggressive return of the Viking warlord, scrambled to respond. King Eadred, who had been preoccupied with consolidating his rule and dealing with internal challenges, was forced to shift his focus to the renewed threat posed by Eirik.

Eadred's response was both strategic and forceful. The king mobilized his forces and began a series of counterattacks against Eirik's positions. The conflict escalated into a series of violent engagements as the two sides clashed in a struggle for control over Northumbria. The fighting was intense and unforgiving, with both sides suffering significant casualties.

Eirik, despite his tactical prowess, faced a formidable challenge. The English forces, bolstered by fresh reinforcements and fortified positions, were determined to repel the Viking invaders. The battle for Northumbria became a fierce and protracted conflict, marked by alternating periods of intense combat and uneasy lulls.

In the midst of this escalating conflict, Eirik met with his closest advisors in a secluded hall within his camp. The atmosphere was tense as the warlord reviewed the latest reports and strategized their next moves. His trusted advisor, Bjorn, spoke up, voicing his concerns.

"Eirik," Bjorn said, his voice tinged with worry, "the English forces are regrouping and strengthening their positions. Our raids have certainly made an impact, but their response is growing more organized. We must consider our next move carefully."

Eirik, his face marked by the strain of continuous warfare, nodded in agreement. "I am aware, Bjorn. Eadred's reinforcements are formidable. We must strike decisively while we still have the element of surprise on our side. If we allow them to consolidate their power, we may lose our advantage."

Bjorn leaned closer, his expression serious. "What if we were to negotiate with some of the local leaders? There are still those who are discontent with Eadred's rule. We could use their support to weaken the English forces further."

Eirik considered this suggestion, his mind racing through the possibilities. "Negotiation could be a viable option, but it must be done with caution. We cannot afford to be seen as weak or desperate. If we can secure allies, it will strengthen our position, but we must ensure their loyalty."

The discussion continued, with Eirik and his advisors debating strategies and potential alliances. As they concluded their meeting, Eirik's resolve was clear. He would pursue both aggressive military action and diplomatic efforts to solidify his position in Northumbria.

One of the significant campaigns during this time was a brutal assault on the fortress of Bamburgh. The fortress, a stronghold of English power in Northumbria, was a key objective for Eirik. The siege was marked by relentless attacks and a sustained effort to breach the fortress's defenses. The fighting was fierce, with both sides engaged in bloody skirmishes and heavy casualties.

Eirik's forces, despite their determination, faced fierce resistance from the English defenders. The siege dragged on for weeks, with Eirik's men enduring the harsh winter weather and the constant threat of counterattacks. Despite their best efforts, the Viking warlord's campaign to capture Bamburgh proved to be a costly and inconclusive endeavor.

As the conflict continued, Eirik's position began to weaken. The English forces, under the leadership of skilled commanders, managed to regain control of several key areas and counter the Viking offensives. The relentless pressure from the English and the logistical challenges of sustaining a prolonged campaign took a toll on Eirik's forces.

The turning point in Eirik's brief resurgence came with the arrival of reinforcements for the English. Eadred, having successfully rallied support from neighboring kingdoms and securing additional military resources, launched a decisive counteroffensive. The reinforcements, combined with the strategic expertise of Eadred's commanders, turned the tide against Eirik's forces.

The final confrontation took place in the spring of 951. Eirik, facing an increasingly formidable English force, made a desperate attempt to secure his position. The battle was fierce and bloody, with both sides fighting with determination and desperation. However, the numerical superiority and strategic advantage of the English forces proved decisive.

Eirik's forces, already exhausted from the prolonged conflict, were overwhelmed by the English onslaught. The battle ended with a decisive victory for Eadred's forces, and Eirik was forced to retreat. The remnants of his once-mighty army scattered, and the Viking warlord was left to face the reality of his defeat.

The aftermath of the battle was marked by a renewed consolidation of English control over Northumbria. Eadred's victory secured his position and restored order to the region. Eirik Bloodaxe, now a defeated and hunted figure, was once again forced to flee.

Eirik's brief resurgence had come to an end. The Viking warlord's attempt to reclaim his throne in Northumbria had been met with fierce opposition and ultimately, overwhelming defeat. The conflict had left a lasting impact on the region, with the echoes of battle and the scars of war serving as a reminder of the turbulent and shifting nature of power.

As Eirik retreated from Northumbria, he faced an uncertain future. His ambitions of reclaiming his former glory had been thwarted, and his position as a warlord was increasingly tenuous. The British Isles, once a land of opportunity, had become a battleground of rival interests and shifting allegiances.

Chapter 20
End of the Axe

The year 952 had begun with a harsh winter across the Pennines, the remote and rugged region that would become the stage for Eirik Bloodaxe's final stand. Eirik, having returned to Northumbria with dreams of reclaiming his lost dominion, found himself facing an increasingly insurmountable challenge. The landscape of power in the British Isles had shifted dramatically, and Eirik's brief resurgence was now overshadowed by the growing strength and resolve of his enemies.

Eirik's position in Northumbria, though once again formidable, was undermined by deep-seated dissent within the region. The Northumbrian nobles, many of whom had initially supported his return, grew increasingly disillusioned with his rule. Their support had been fickle, driven by opportunism rather than loyalty. As Eirik's campaigns stretched on and the toll of constant warfare mounted, the nobles began to see an opportunity to rid themselves of the Viking warlord and secure their own futures under English control.

The betrayal began to unfold with subtlety and treachery. The Northumbrian nobles, seeking to align themselves with the rising power of the English king, Eadred, began to secretly negotiate with his representatives. Their aim was to shift their allegiance and ensure their own positions of power and influence in the new political order.

Eirik, ever perceptive to the shifting tides, grew increasingly suspicious of the nobles' motives. His once-loyal advisors began to voice their concerns, noting the signs of discontent and the growing distance between Eirik and his Northumbrian allies. Despite his efforts to address these issues, the situation deteriorated rapidly.

In a secluded chamber within his camp, Eirik convened a meeting with his closest advisors. The room was dimly lit, the flickering light of torches casting shadows on the walls as the air thickened with tension.

"I have received troubling reports," Eirik said, his voice low and intense. "It seems our allies within Northumbria are growing distant. There are whispers of their shifting loyalties, and I fear we may face betrayal from within."

His advisor, Gunnar, a grizzled veteran of many battles, spoke up. "Eirik, it's clear that the nobles are seeking to align themselves with Eadred. Their ambitions are driven by self-interest, and they see an opportunity to secure their own futures. We must act swiftly to address this threat."

Eirik's expression darkened. "We cannot afford to be caught off guard. If the nobles turn against us, we will be left vulnerable. We need to consolidate our position and make our intentions clear. I will not let Northumbria slip from our grasp without a fight."

The conversation continued as Eirik and his advisors debated their options and strategies. Despite their efforts to address the brewing discontent, the situation was rapidly deteriorating. The Northumbrian nobles, having secured their pact with Eadred, began to take more overt actions against Eirik's forces.

The final confrontation occurred at the Battle of Stainmore, a remote and desolate region in the Pennines. The battle was a desperate and brutal engagement, set against the backdrop of the harsh winter landscape. Eirik's forces, though battle-hardened, faced a formidable coalition of English troops and Northumbrian rebels.

As the two sides prepared for the clash, the air was thick with anticipation and dread. Eirik, mounted on his horse and clad in battle-worn armor, surveyed the battlefield with grim determination. His loyal followers, though weary, stood ready for the fight.

The battle began with a ferocious assault. Eirik's forces, despite their fighting spirit, were met with a coordinated and relentless attack from the English and their Northumbrian allies. The terrain, icy and treacherous, added to the difficulty of the combat. The clash of weapons and the cries of battle echoed across the bleak landscape.

Amidst the chaos, Eirik found himself face-to-face with the leaders of the Northumbrian rebels. The confrontation was tense and fraught with emotion. Eirik's expression, though resolute, betrayed a flicker of betrayal and anguish.

"Why?" Eirik shouted over the din of battle. "Why have you turned against me? We fought together. I gave you power and protection."

One of the Northumbrian leaders, a noble named Aethelwynn, met Eirik's gaze with a mixture of defiance and regret. "Eirik, you have been a great warrior, but your rule brought only strife and bloodshed. We have chosen a future aligned with King Eadred, one of stability and peace."

Eirik's eyes flashed with anger and betrayal. "Stability? Peace? You seek only to save your own skins. You will never find true peace while serving the English. This land has been soaked in our blood, and now you abandon it to the enemy."

The battle raged on, with Eirik's forces struggling to hold their ground. The combined might of the English and the Northumbrian rebels proved overwhelming. Despite his efforts and valor, Eirik's position was increasingly untenable.

As the tide of battle turned against him, Eirik fought with relentless fury. His enemies pressed their advantage, and the battle became a desperate struggle for survival. Eirik's forces, exhausted and outnumbered, began to falter.

In the midst of the chaos, Eirik's final stand came as a dramatic culmination of his relentless quest for power. As the enemy closed in, Eirik's thoughts turned to his legacy and the tumultuous path he had followed. The final moments were marked by a fierce and defiant resistance, a testament to his indomitable spirit even in the face of defeat.

In his last moments, Eirik was surrounded by his loyal warriors. His voice, though strained, carried a sense of defiant finality. "Let it be known that Eirik Bloodaxe fought to the end for what he believed in. Our struggle was not in vain. The blood spilled here will not be forgotten. Remember us, and remember that we stood against the tide."

As the battle drew to a close, Eirik Bloodaxe fell on the icy battlefield of Stainmore. The once-feared Viking warlord, who had carved a path of violence and ambition through the British Isles, lay defeated.

His death marked the end of Viking rule in Northumbria and signaled the final incorporation of the kingdom into England.

The legacy of Eirik Bloodaxe would endure as a poignant chapter in the history of the British Isles. His rise and fall, marked by both fierce ambition and tragic betrayal, served as a reminder of the turbulent nature of power and the relentless forces that shape the course of history. The once-mighty Viking warlord had met his end, and with it, the era of Viking dominance in Northumbria came to a decisive and somber close.

The Legend: Demystified

Outline:

I. Introduction

- **Background and Context:**
    - Eirik Bloodaxe (Old Norse: Eiríkr blóðøx) was a Viking warlord and one of Harald Fairhair's many sons.
    - His name reflects his violent exploits and association with warfare.
    - Eirik's life spanned the late 9th century into the early 10th century, and his reigns over Norway and Northumbria were brief but significant.
    - Sources include the sagas, skaldic poetry, Anglo-Saxon Chronicles, and archaeological findings, though accounts vary.

II. Early Life

- **Birth and Family Background:**
    - Born circa 885 AD, one of the many sons of Harald Fairhair, the first King of Norway.

- His mother was Ragnhild Eriksdatter, one of Harald's many wives.
- Raised in a warrior culture, Eirik was taught the arts of war from an early age.
- **Harald Fairhair's Kingdom:**
  - Harald's effort to consolidate Norway created numerous rivalries between his sons.
  - Eirik's early exposure to conflict shaped his future ambition to claim kingship.

III. Rise to Power in Norway

- **Early Exploits:**
  - Eirik's first military campaigns involved Viking raids and skirmishes in the British Isles and the Baltic region.
  - His early adventures earned him the nickname "Bloodaxe" due to his brutality in battle.
- **Claim to the Throne:**
  - Upon Harald Fairhair's death or abdication (around 930 AD), Norway was divided among Harald's many sons.
  - Eirik sought to become the sole ruler, killing several of his brothers,

including Ragnvald and Olaf, to eliminate rivals.

- **Brief Reign as King of Norway (930-934 AD):**
    - His reign over Norway was marked by violence, instability, and growing opposition.
    - Eirik's rule was unpopular due to his harsh governance and the bloodshed he inflicted upon his kin.
    - He was eventually driven out by his younger half-brother Haakon the Good, who had returned from England with Christian support.

IV. Exile and Reign in Northumbria

- **Exile in the British Isles:**
    - After his expulsion from Norway, Eirik became a warlord in the British Isles, continuing his Viking raiding.
    - He aligned himself with the Kingdom of Northumbria, a region with a Viking influence.
- **First Reign as King of Northumbria (947-948 AD):**
    - Eirik was invited by Northumbrian nobles to rule, hoping he could defend the kingdom against Scots and other threats.

- His first reign was short-lived, and he was ousted after a year by the Anglo-Saxon king Eadred, who sought control of Northumbria.
- **Return and Second Reign (952-954 AD):**
  - Eirik returned to Northumbria and regained the throne for a brief period.
  - His reign was again marked by violent campaigns against rivals and opposition from the English.
- **Conflict with Eadred of Wessex:**
  - Eadred launched a campaign to reassert control over Northumbria.
  - Eirik's supporters dwindled, leading to internal instability.

V. Death and Legacy

- **Death (circa 954 AD):**
  - Eirik was betrayed by Northumbrian nobles and killed at the Battle of Stainmore, a remote region in the Pennines.
  - His death marked the end of Viking rule in Northumbria and the final incorporation of the kingdom into England.
- **Legacy in the Sagas and Viking Lore:**
  - Eirik Bloodaxe is remembered in various sagas, including

"Heimskringla" by Snorri Sturluson,
which paints him as a fierce warrior
but ultimately tragic figure.

- Skaldic poetry like *Eiríksmál*
  celebrated him as a great warrior
  welcomed into Valhalla.
- His legacy as a king is
  overshadowed by his violent and
  chaotic rule, though he is
  remembered as a symbol of Viking
  ferocity.

VI. Historical Debate and Myth

- **Contradictory Sources:**
  - Eirik's portrayal in sources varies,
    with some medieval chronicles
    portraying him as a villain, while
    sagas romanticize his reign.
  - The nickname "Bloodaxe" has been
    debated, with some historians
    suggesting it was exaggerated in
    later centuries.
- **Eirik's Importance in Viking History:**
  - His life reflects the turbulent period
    of Viking expansion, internal family
    conflict, and the eventual
    Christianization of Scandinavia.
  - His struggle for power represents
    the decline of traditional Viking rulers

as they clashed with emerging Christian monarchies.

VII. Conclusion

- **End of the Viking Era in Britain:**
    - Eirik's death marked a significant turning point in the transition from Viking dominance to Anglo-Saxon consolidation.
- **Cultural Impact:**
    - The enduring fascination with Eirik Bloodaxe's life, both as a brutal warrior and tragic king, continues to shape Viking mythology.
    - His story is emblematic of the violent struggles for power that defined early medieval Scandinavian and British history.

Introduction

Eirik Bloodaxe, a name synonymous with ferocity and ambition, was born around 885 AD to Harald Fairhair, the first King of Norway. Eirik's life was intricately entwined with the larger narrative of Viking expansion and consolidation, and his early years provide crucial context for understanding his later exploits and turbulent reigns.

Harald Fairhair, Eirik's father, was a seminal figure in Norwegian history. His reign marked a pivotal era in the unification of Norway. Before Harald's ascendancy, Norway was a patchwork of independent chiefdoms and tribes, each with its own local rulers. Harald's vision of a unified Norway drove his relentless campaign to consolidate these disparate regions under a single banner. His efforts to centralize power were met with resistance and conflict, but his eventual success established him as the first king of a unified Norway.

Harald's consolidation of power was not merely a matter of military conquest but also involved intricate family dynamics. As he worked to unify Norway, Harald accumulated a considerable number of wives and concubines, resulting in numerous offspring. Eirik Bloodaxe was one of his many sons, born to Ragnhild Eriksdatter, one of Harald's wives. Ragnhild's background was significant in her own right, and her marriage to Harald was part of the broader political strategy to secure alliances and strengthen Harald's claim to kingship.

From the moment of his birth, Eirik was destined to be a part of this ambitious and often volatile royal family. His early life was shaped by the intense rivalries and power struggles that characterized his father's efforts to create a cohesive kingdom. The court of Harald Fairhair was a place of both grandeur and tension, as the king's multiple sons, each with their own claims and aspirations, navigated a complex web of familial competition.

Harald's kingdom, at the time of Eirik's birth, was undergoing a significant transformation. The process of unification was far from complete, and the kingdom was often in flux. Harald's rule was marked by a series of conflicts with local chieftains and rival factions who resisted his centralizing efforts. These battles were not just physical confrontations but also deeply embedded in the social and political fabric of Viking society.

Eirik's upbringing in this environment was one of preparation for the harsh realities of Viking life. Raised amidst the warrior culture that defined his father's reign, Eirik was schooled in the arts of combat and leadership from an early age. The skills and attitudes he acquired during his formative years were reflective of the broader Viking ethos: valor in battle, ambition, and a relentless pursuit of power.

The internal dynamics within Harald's family also played a crucial role in shaping Eirik's future. The king's numerous children were not merely symbolic heirs but active participants in the political and military affairs of the realm. Eirik's position as one of Harald's sons placed him in direct competition with his siblings, a situation that would later influence his own quest for power. The rivalries among Harald's offspring were not just familial but had significant implications for the governance and stability of Norway.

As Harald Fairhair's kingdom expanded and solidified, it became a formidable power in Scandinavia. The unification of Norway under Harald's rule was a significant achievement, but it also sowed the seeds of future conflict. The consolidation efforts created a complex political landscape, characterized by shifting alliances and ongoing rivalries. For Eirik Bloodaxe, growing up in this environment meant learning to navigate a world of political intrigue and martial prowess.

In summary, Eirik Bloodaxe's birth and early life were deeply intertwined with the ambitions and challenges faced by his father, Harald Fairhair. Raised in a kingdom undergoing transformation and shaped by familial rivalries, Eirik's early years set the stage for his later actions and aspirations. The kingdom that Harald Fairhair built was one of both opportunity and conflict, providing a tumultuous backdrop for the life of Eirik Bloodaxe and his eventual rise to power.

Early Life

Eirik Bloodaxe's early life was steeped in the rugged realities of Viking culture, characterized by intense martial training and the intricate dynamics of his royal family. Born around 885 AD, Eirik was the son of Harald Fairhair, the pioneering king who sought to unify Norway from a mosaic of independent chieftaincies. His upbringing was meticulously designed to prepare him for a life of warfare and leadership, mirroring the broader values and challenges of Viking society.

From the moment of his birth, Eirik was placed into an environment where strength, valor, and martial prowess were highly esteemed. The Viking world was one where the skills of a warrior were not just an aspect of life but its very essence. This emphasis on combat and leadership was not an arbitrary choice but a necessity in a society frequently engaged in conflicts and raiding expeditions.

Eirik's early training in the arts of war began as soon as he could walk. In the Viking tradition, warrior training started at a young age, and Eirik was no exception. Raised in a royal household where martial skills were prized, he was taught the fundamentals of combat almost from the cradle. His education was not limited to mere physical training but encompassed a comprehensive understanding of strategy, tactics, and the cultural significance of warfare.

Under the guidance of his father and other seasoned warriors in Harald Fairhair's court, Eirik learned to handle weapons with skill and precision. The training was rigorous and designed to test both his physical endurance and his mental fortitude. By the time he reached adolescence, Eirik would have been proficient with a range of weapons, including the axe, sword, and spear, tools essential for the Viking raider and chieftain. The axe, in particular, became emblematic of his later moniker, "Bloodaxe," reflecting his reputation for ruthless efficiency in battle.

In addition to physical training, Eirik was educated in the art of strategy. The Vikings valued cunning and tactical acumen as much as brute strength. Eirik's education would have included lessons in battlefield tactics, siege warfare, and naval engagements. The latter was particularly crucial, given the Viking emphasis on seafaring and the frequent use of longships for both raiding and exploration. Understanding how to navigate and utilize these vessels effectively was an integral part of his preparation for leadership and warfare.

The cultural and psychological aspects of warfare were also a significant part of Eirik's early training. The Viking ethos celebrated bravery and honor, and young warriors were instilled with a sense of destiny and duty. The sagas and skaldic poetry of the time often recounted heroic deeds and the valor of great warriors, creating a narrative that Eirik was expected to emulate. This cultural backdrop added a layer of psychological pressure, as living up to the legendary standards set by his forebears and peers was both a personal and societal expectation.

Eirik's familial environment was equally influential in shaping his approach to warfare. The Viking age was a time of intense familial rivalry, and the sons of Harald Fairhair were no exception. Growing up in such a competitive atmosphere, where siblings often vied for favor and power, Eirik would have been acutely aware of the need to distinguish himself through martial prowess and strategic acumen. The competition among Harald's sons for control over different parts of Norway further sharpened Eirik's focus on developing his skills.

The influence of his mother, Ragnhild Eriksdatter, also played a role in Eirik's upbringing. While less documented than Harald's influence, Ragnhild's position and background would have contributed to the broader cultural and political education Eirik received. Her support and guidance, while secondary to Harald's direct instruction, were nonetheless part of the framework that shaped Eirik's early years.

Rise to Power in Norway

Eirik Bloodaxe's ascent to power in Norway is a tale marked by ambition, strategic acumen, and ruthless determination. His rise to prominence was not merely a product of his martial prowess but also a reflection of the turbulent political landscape of 10th-century Scandinavia, shaped by familial rivalries and the broader process of unification under his father, Harald Fairhair.

Born around 885 AD, Eirik was the son of Harald Fairhair, the king who sought to unify Norway from a fragmented collection of chieftaincies. Harald's ambition to centralize authority and consolidate control over the disparate regions of Norway created a complex and often volatile political environment. This environment set the stage for Eirik's eventual rise to power, a process marked by both strategic maneuvering and brutal conflict.

As a young man, Eirik was immersed in the art of warfare and leadership, taught to handle weapons and lead men with a combination of skill and ferocity. The early lessons he received from his father and other seasoned warriors laid the groundwork for his later actions. His reputation as a fierce and capable fighter, coupled with his deep understanding of Viking warfare, positioned him as a formidable contender for power.

Upon Harald Fairhair's death, which occurred around 930 AD, Norway was divided among his numerous sons. This division was both a testament to Harald's achievements and a source of significant conflict. The kingdom's fragmentation into several territories meant that each son, including Eirik, was granted a share of the realm to govern. The distribution of power among Harald's offspring inevitably led to rivalries and disputes over dominance.

Eirik's ambition was evident from the outset. Unlike some of his siblings, who accepted their assigned territories with relative contentment, Eirik sought to extend his influence and control over a larger portion of Norway. His determination to become the sole ruler drove him to take drastic measures. In a series of brutal moves, Eirik eliminated several of his brothers, including Ragnvald and Olaf. These actions were part of a larger strategy to consolidate power and remove rivals, reflecting a ruthless streak that would characterize much of his career.

Eirik's initial rise to power was marked by a series of military campaigns designed to assert his dominance. These campaigns were not merely about expanding territory but were also strategic moves to weaken the positions of his rivals and solidify his control over Norway. Eirik's military prowess was matched by his ability to leverage alliances and exploit the existing power structures to his advantage.

His reign over Norway, which began around 930 AD and lasted until 934 AD, was characterized by a tumultuous and often violent period. Eirik's rule was marked by a series of internal conflicts and uprisings, driven by both external threats and internal dissent. The harshness of his governance and the bloodshed inflicted upon his rivals created a climate of instability and unrest. Eirik's approach to leadership, while effective in consolidating power, was also alienating, leading to growing opposition from both within and outside his realm.

One of the key factors in Eirik's rise was his ability to harness the Viking tradition of raiding and warfare. The Vikings were known for their seafaring prowess and their capacity to conduct swift and devastating raids. Eirik utilized these capabilities to his advantage, engaging in both raids and military campaigns that served to enhance his reputation and strengthen his position. His actions were not just about expanding territory but were also strategic moves to demonstrate his power and assert his dominance.

The consolidation of power by Eirik was ultimately challenged by his half-brother Haakon the Good, who had returned from England with Christian support. Haakon's return marked a significant turning point in the political landscape of Norway. His support from Christian factions provided him with a valuable base of power and legitimacy that Eirik could not match. The ensuing conflict between Eirik and Haakon was both a struggle for control over Norway and a clash of differing visions for the kingdom's future.

Eirik's downfall was a result of a combination of internal dissent and external pressures. His reign, though marked by significant achievements and a formidable display of power, was ultimately unsustainable. The growing opposition, coupled with Haakon's successful return and consolidation of support, led to Eirik's eventual expulsion from Norway.

In the broader context of Norwegian history, Eirik Bloodaxe's rise to power was a reflection of the complex dynamics of Viking society, characterized by intense rivalries, shifting alliances, and the relentless pursuit of dominance. His ability to rise to prominence amidst such turmoil speaks to his strategic acumen and martial skill. However, the very qualities that enabled his ascent also contributed to his downfall, as the volatility of his rule and the harshness of his governance led to widespread opposition and ultimately, his expulsion from Norway.

Eirik's ascent to power was a dramatic episode in the history of Norway, illustrating the fierce competition and dynamic political landscape of the Viking Age. His story, marked by both impressive achievements and tragic flaws, serves as a testament to the tumultuous nature of Viking politics and the relentless quest for power that defined the era.

Exile and Reign in Northumbria

Eirik Bloodaxe's journey from Norway to the British Isles represents a dramatic chapter in the tumultuous history of Viking expansion and power struggles. After being ousted from Norway, Eirik's exile led him to seek new opportunities across the North Sea. His subsequent rise to power in Northumbria, a region of strategic significance in the British Isles, highlights his relentless ambition and the complex interplay of Viking and Anglo-Saxon politics.

Following his expulsion from Norway, Eirik Bloodaxe found himself in a precarious position. His ambitions had been thwarted by his half-brother Haakon the Good, and his hold on Norway was irreversibly weakened. Eirik, however, was not one to accept defeat quietly. His exile was not a period of idle reflection but rather a time of active seeking and opportunity. The British Isles, with their fragmented political landscape and frequent conflicts, presented a fertile ground for a warlord of Eirik's stature.

By the mid-940s, Eirik had successfully reoriented his focus towards the Kingdom of Northumbria, a region with a significant Viking presence. Northumbria was a crucial territory, strategically located in the north of England, and had been a focal point for Viking raiding and settlement. The kingdom had been under the control of various Viking leaders, and its political instability made it an attractive target for someone like Eirik who was eager to reassert his dominance.

Eirik's initial foray into Northumbria was marked by his alignment with the local Viking factions. The Northumbrian nobles, facing threats from both English forces and internal dissent, saw in Eirik a powerful ally who could provide military strength and leadership. In 947 AD, Eirik was invited to take up the throne of Northumbria, a position that offered him the opportunity to regain some of his lost prestige and influence. His first reign, however, was short-lived. Within a year, in 948 AD, Eirik was overthrown by King Eadred of Wessex, who sought to consolidate control over the northern territories.

Eadred's campaign against Northumbria was part of a broader strategy to assert English dominance over the northern regions. Eirik's brief tenure as king highlighted the tenuous nature of Viking control in the area and the shifting balance of power between Viking and Anglo-Saxon forces. Eadred's successful campaign effectively ousted

Eirik and reasserted English control over Northumbria, pushing Eirik into another phase of exile.

Yet Eirik's story did not end with his ousting. The Viking warlord's resilience was evident as he regrouped and sought to reclaim his position. By 952 AD, Eirik had managed to return to Northumbria. His second stint as king was marked by a renewed sense of determination and aggression. Eirik's reign during this period was characterized by a series of violent campaigns against both his rivals within Northumbria and the encroaching English forces. His efforts to consolidate power were relentless, and he sought to reestablish his control over the kingdom with the same ruthlessness that had defined his earlier career.

Despite his vigorous efforts, Eirik's second reign was plagued by internal strife and external opposition. The Northumbrian nobles, who had initially supported him, began to waver in their loyalty. The political landscape was increasingly unstable, with competing factions and the persistent threat of English intervention. Eadred of Wessex, determined to secure his control over Northumbria, launched another campaign to reclaim the territory and neutralize the threat posed by Eirik.

In 954 AD, the conflict culminated in the Battle of Stainmore, a decisive confrontation that would mark the end of Eirik Bloodaxe's attempts to secure a lasting foothold in the British Isles. The Battle of Stainmore, fought in the remote Pennine region, was a crucial engagement in the struggle between the Viking and Anglo-Saxon forces. Eirik was ultimately betrayed by some of the Northumbrian nobles who had once supported him. This betrayal, combined with the superior military strategy and strength of Eadred's forces, led to Eirik's defeat and death.

The Battle of Stainmore was a turning point, not just for Eirik but for the broader historical context of Viking rule in Northumbria. Eirik's death in the aftermath of the battle marked the final end of Viking dominance in the region. Northumbria was fully incorporated into the growing English kingdom, and the era of Viking kingship in the British Isles drew to a close.

Death and Legacy

The death of Eirik Bloodaxe in 954 marked a significant turning point in the history of Viking rule in the British Isles and the wider Viking expansion into the territories of the British Isles. His death was not merely a personal tragedy but a pivotal moment in the broader historical narrative, signaling the end of an era of Viking dominance in Northumbria and the final incorporation of the kingdom into the expanding English realm.

Eirik Bloodaxe met his end at the Battle of Stainmore, a remote and strategically important location in the Pennines, a range of hills that formed a natural barrier between the North and the South of England. The battle itself was the culmination of a series of intense conflicts between Eirik and the forces loyal to King Eadred of Wessex. The outcome of the battle was decisively in favor of Eadred, whose forces were better coordinated and more resolute in their campaign to reassert control over Northumbria.

The battle was not just a clash of armies but a confrontation between two fundamentally opposed visions for the future of the North of England. Eirik, with his fierce ambition and ruthless tactics, represented the last vestiges of Viking authority in the region. His death symbolized the end of the Viking era in Northumbria, a period characterized by intermittent Viking control and frequent conflicts with the Anglo-Saxon kingdoms. With Eirik's demise, the Anglo-Saxons were able to solidify their control over Northumbria, integrating it fully into the kingdom of England.

Following Eirik's death, the immediate aftermath was a consolidation of English power in the North. The English Crown, under Eadred, moved quickly to ensure that Viking influence in the region was eliminated. The remnants of Viking resistance were quelled, and the political landscape was restructured to reinforce English authority. Northumbria, once a stronghold of Viking power, was effectively absorbed into the expanding English kingdom, marking a significant shift in the balance of power in the British Isles.

Eirik Bloodaxe's legacy, as seen through the lens of history, is a complex one. He is remembered as one of the most formidable and controversial figures of the Viking Age. His reputation as a warrior and a leader was marked by both fear and respect. The sagas and chronicles that recount his life often depict him as a fierce and ruthless ruler, emphasizing his reputation for violence and his relentless pursuit of power. The nickname "Bloodaxe," which he acquired due to his brutal nature in battle, reflects this image and has become emblematic of his legacy.

In the Norse sagas, such as the "Heimskringla" by Snorri Sturluson, Eirik is portrayed as a tragic hero, a warrior whose life and death were shaped by the harsh realities of his time. These accounts often romanticize his achievements and struggles, presenting him as a figure caught between the ideals of Viking heroism and the inevitability of his downfall. The sagas highlight his valor in battle and his determination to reclaim his lost power, painting a picture of a man who, despite his flaws, was a significant and influential figure in Viking history.

Eirik's legacy was also shaped by the poetic traditions of the time. Skaldic poetry, which celebrated the deeds of notable figures, often included references to Eirik's prowess and his eventual fate. These poems contributed to his lasting image as a great warrior who met a tragic end, reinforcing the narrative of his heroism and his dramatic downfall.

Despite the valorized accounts, Eirik Bloodaxe's rule and subsequent death also serve as a reminder of the volatility and brutality of the Viking Age. His efforts to regain power after being expelled from Norway illustrate the relentless nature of Viking leadership and the fierce competition for dominance that characterized the period. His eventual defeat and death at Stainmore marked the end of an era of Viking hegemony in Northumbria, a region that had been a focal point of Viking expansion and conflict.

The broader historical impact of Eirik's death was significant. It marked the final stage of Viking attempts to exert control over the British Isles, and the incorporation of Northumbria into the English kingdom signified a key moment in the consolidation of English power. The absorption of Northumbria into England was a critical step in the eventual unification of England under a single monarch, paving the way for the later medieval period.

Historical Debate and Myth

The historical figure of Eirik Bloodaxe has long been a subject of intrigue and debate, with his name and legacy shrouded in a blend of historical fact, myth, and interpretative variations. His moniker, "Bloodaxe," is particularly emblematic of the complexities surrounding his historical portrayal and the subsequent myths that have grown around his name.

The name "Bloodaxe" itself is a point of significant historical debate. It is commonly believed that the moniker was not Eirik's original surname but rather a descriptive epithet given to him due to his brutal and bloody approach to warfare. In Old Norse, "blóðøx" can be translated to "blood axe," suggesting a figure whose actions were marked by extreme violence and savagery. This nickname reflects the Viking custom of assigning descriptive names that encapsulated a person's deeds or character traits. However, the origins and accuracy of this epithet are subject to scholarly scrutiny and interpretation.

The historical sources that mention Eirik Bloodaxe include the sagas, such as the "Heimskringla" by Snorri Sturluson, and various medieval chronicles and annals. These sources often depict Eirik in a dramatic light, emphasizing his fierce nature and violent rule. For instance, Snorri Sturluson's "Heimskringla," a collection of sagas that chronicles the lives of Norse kings, portrays Eirik as a formidable and ruthless warrior, highlighting his prowess in battle and his turbulent reign. This portrayal aligns with the nickname "Bloodaxe," reinforcing the image of a fearsome and uncompromising leader.

However, the sagas and medieval accounts are not without their biases and embellishments. They were written centuries after the events they describe and often serve to reflect the values, perspectives, and agendas of their authors rather than providing an objective historical record. In the case of Eirik, the sagas were composed in a context where heroic and dramatic portrayals of Viking leaders were common. The emphasis on his brutality and the moniker "Bloodaxe" may therefore be more reflective of literary and cultural traditions than of a historically accurate assessment of his character.

The historical accuracy of the name "Bloodaxe" is further complicated by the varying accounts of Eirik's life. Some sources suggest that the epithet was not used during his lifetime but was attributed to him later as a means of encapsulating his legacy. The name could have been a later addition by historians or poets who sought to frame Eirik's actions within a specific narrative of Viking heroism and brutality. This retrospective attribution raises questions about how much of Eirik's legacy was shaped by later interpretations versus contemporary reality.

In addition to the name itself, the myths surrounding Eirik Bloodaxe contribute to the broader historical debate. The sagas often blend historical events with mythological elements, creating a narrative that is both compelling and problematic for historians seeking to separate fact from fiction. Eirik's depiction as a tragic hero, marked by both great achievements and dramatic failures, serves to enhance the dramatic effect of the stories rather than provide a straightforward historical account.

Another aspect of the mythologization of Eirik Bloodaxe is the role of skaldic poetry. Skaldic poems, which celebrated the deeds of Norse kings and warriors, frequently included references to Eirik. These poems, composed by court poets known as skalds, were designed to glorify their patrons and immortalize their deeds. While they provide valuable insights into the cultural perception of Eirik, they also contribute to the mythological layer of his legacy. The praise and accolades in skaldic poetry can be seen as a way of reinforcing the heroic and fearsome image of Eirik, rather than providing a balanced historical assessment.

The historical debate around Eirik Bloodaxe's name and legacy illustrates the challenges faced by historians in reconstructing the past. The blending of historical fact with literary embellishment, combined with the evolving interpretations of his deeds, creates a complex portrait of a figure whose true nature remains elusive. The moniker "Bloodaxe," while evocative, may not fully capture the nuances of Eirik's reign and character. It represents both the dramatic flair of historical narratives and the difficulty of distinguishing between historical reality and mythological representation.

Ultimately, the name "Bloodaxe" and the myths surrounding Eirik Bloodaxe reflect broader themes in Viking history and historiography. They underscore the impact of narrative and interpretation in shaping our understanding of historical figures and highlight the ways in which legends and epithets can both reveal and obscure the complexities of the past. Eirik's story, with its mix of violence, ambition, and eventual downfall, continues to captivate and challenge historians and enthusiasts alike, serving as a powerful example of the interplay between history and myth.

Conclusion

Eirik Bloodaxe's legacy as a brutal warrior and king has left a significant imprint on Viking mythology and cultural memory, shaping how we understand the Viking Age and its leaders. His life and reputation reflect the broader cultural and historical narratives of the time, and his influence extends into modern perceptions of Viking heroism and villainy.

The cultural impact of Eirik Bloodaxe is primarily evident through the lens of Viking sagas and skaldic poetry. These literary forms, which emerged from the oral traditions of the Norse people, played a crucial role in shaping the mythological and historical narratives surrounding figures like Eirik. The sagas, such as Snorri Sturluson's "Heimskringla," depict Eirik as a formidable and fearsome leader, emphasizing his military prowess and his often brutal methods. This portrayal contributed to the creation of a larger-than-life image of Eirik that has resonated through the centuries.

The depiction of Eirik in the sagas reflects the values and ideals of Norse culture, where qualities such as strength, bravery, and ruthlessness were highly esteemed. The sagas present Eirik as a warrior who epitomized these traits, reinforcing the notion of the Viking leader as a figure of immense power and intimidation. His nickname, "Bloodaxe," encapsulates the essence of this portrayal, highlighting the brutal nature of his rule and his reputation for violence. This image has become a symbol of the Viking Age's dramatic and often violent history.

Skaldic poetry also played a significant role in shaping Eirik's legacy. Skalds, the poets of the Norse courts, composed elaborate verses celebrating the deeds of their patrons. These poems often highlighted the heroism and valor of Viking leaders, contributing to their mythological status. Eirik's exploits were celebrated in skaldic poems, which emphasized his martial skill and his dramatic struggles for power. The poetic tradition helped to immortalize Eirik's achievements and his turbulent reign, embedding his story into the cultural consciousness of the Norse people.

The impact of Eirik Bloodaxe on Viking mythology extends beyond his own time and into modern interpretations of Viking history. His life and legacy have been the subject of extensive historical and literary analysis, influencing how we perceive Viking culture and leadership. Eirik's story, with its blend of heroism and brutality, has contributed to the enduring fascination with Viking warriors and their complex personalities. His dramatic rise and fall, coupled with his fearsome reputation, have become archetypal elements in the narrative of the Viking Age.

Modern popular culture has also been influenced by Eirik's legacy. The image of Eirik Bloodaxe as a ruthless and powerful figure has been adopted and adapted in various forms of media, including literature, film, and television. His character often serves as a representation of the archetypal Viking warrior, embodying the fierce and uncompromising traits that are commonly associated with Viking mythology. This portrayal reflects both the historical reality of Viking leadership and the romanticized versions of Viking life that have emerged over time.

Eirik's impact on Viking mythology is also evident in the way his story has been woven into broader historical and cultural narratives. The themes of power, betrayal, and downfall that characterize his life resonate with the larger patterns of Viking history and mythology. His dramatic life and death have become emblematic of the tumultuous nature of Viking rule and the struggles for dominance that defined the era. Eirik's story reflects the broader cultural fascination with Viking heroism and the complex interplay of violence, ambition, and fate.

Furthermore, the ongoing interest in Eirik Bloodaxe and his legacy highlights the broader cultural and historical significance of Viking figures in contemporary society. The enduring fascination with Viking history and mythology, fueled by figures like Eirik, reflects a continued fascination with the dramatic and often violent aspects of the Viking Age. Eirik's story serves as a powerful example of how historical figures can shape cultural narratives and influence modern perceptions of the past.

In summary, Eirik Bloodaxe's cultural impact as a brutal warrior and king is a testament to the enduring legacy of Viking mythology. His life and reputation have been shaped by the sagas, skaldic poetry, and subsequent historical interpretations, creating a complex and multifaceted portrait of a figure who continues to captivate and intrigue. The myths and stories surrounding Eirik reflect the values and ideals of the Viking Age, while also influencing contemporary understandings of Viking history and culture. His legacy, as both a fearsome leader and a symbol of Viking heroism, continues to resonate in modern depictions of the Viking Age, highlighting the enduring power of myth and narrative in shaping our understanding of history.

Don't miss the next book in the Viking Saga series,

The Heavy Hand
of Harald Hardrada

IF YOU'VE ENJOYED THIS BOOK,

Please consider leaving an honest review at your favorite online book retailer. It's like sending a cookie to the author without having to spend a penny.